monsoonbooks

WRITTEN IN BLACK

KH Lim was born and raised in Brunei. He attended medical school in the UK and qualified in 2008.

When he isn't pretending to be an author, he works as a doctor in Singapore, where he currently resides.

Written in Black

KH Lim

monsoon

monsoonbooks

Published in 2014
by Monsoon Books Pte Ltd
www.monsoonbooks.com.sg

Editorial / Sales:
No.1 Duke of Windsor Suite, Burrough Court, Burrough on the Hill,
Leics. LE14 2QS, UK

Registered office:
150 Orchard Road #07-02, Singapore 238841

First edition.

ISBN (paperback): 978-981-4423-97-7
ISBN (ebook): 978-981-4423-98-4

Cover design by Cover Kitchen.

Printed in the United States
16 15 14 1 2 3 4 5

In memory of the real *Ah Kongs*

Chapter One

It was a Tuesday morning when I got the call from my uncle, catching me at the very moment I was about to decide which of my two blue pens I was going to resign myself to using over my favoured black one. There was work to be done, and a certain way I had to do it, and I'd already wasted much of the afternoon with my face buried in my tattered six-year-old copy of *Huckleberry Finn*.

Ah Peh sounded like he had a bad cold as he asked where my father was. I told him what I knew, which was that I didn't know where my father was or when he would be back home. My uncle then grumbled about Pa always leaving his mobile phone switched off. I interrupted to ask if it was anything urgent before he could say his curt goodbye and hang up on me.

"Urgent? Boy, your *Ah Kong* won't be there anymore when your father arrives."

"Oh, so you finally managed to get him moved to a better place?"

"Jonathan, don't ..."

"Down to the warmer rooms? You know, with his cough ..."

"Jonathan, stop! Listen to me. Your *Ah Kong* is gone. Do you understand? He's gone."

"Ah." I was too surprised to say anything else, and remained holding the phone to my ear long after my uncle had hung up. When the disconnect tone turned into a deafeningly shrill squeal in my right ear, I was finally snapped out of it. I knew my grandfather had been admitted at the hospital two days ago for a bad chest, but Pa had never let on how poorly *Ah Kong* had been doing. He'd even kept us kids from going over to visit him, telling us to concentrate on more pressing matters, like our upcoming tests and assignment deadlines.

And now *Ah Kong* was well and truly gone, for good. Yet, somehow, the only thing I could think about at that moment was how our family gatherings would be a lot less troublesome from now on. I wouldn't have to worry anymore about getting badgered into massaging his dusty old feet, with their hard, crooked, yellow nails and flaking bits of skin. Or lighting him cigarettes behind my parents' backs. Or getting dragged along to visit his grizzled coffee-stall buddies, who loved to ask me weird questions about which side of my family I preferred or how many houses my mother's family owned or which of my mother's cousins had been out of work the longest.

When Pa eventually returned home, it was in one hell of a huff: sweaty, red-faced, his clothes dishevelled and Mum's ill-fitting sunglasses slipping off the near-non-existent bridge of his nose. The sight of my father in such a state felt far more disconcerting than finding out my grandfather had just died; I'd rarely seen him as flustered as he was now when he shambled up the stairs and into the open area, where I was sitting on the sofa finishing off *Huckleberry Finn* whilst picking out with my free hand the yellowing sponge of the sofa's innards through its rips.

Bound by our respective rooms and the staircase entry, the open area could barely accommodate two cupboards – which were stuffed with old novels, magazines and souvenirs from my parents' past, like their various sports- and dance trophies and their trinkets from their travels in Europe – a couple of creaky sofas and uncushioned rattan armchairs, and a fusty old TV with its screen made of hard glass and with only the lower half of what remained of its adjustable antenna.

There was nothing from Pa as he brushed past all this (including my ten-year-old self, since I probably counted as one of the fixtures to him for all intents and purposes) then slammed the door of his room shut behind him. I felt the reverberations rattle the dingy old couch I was lounging on, and flakes of paint fell onto the floor since the slam had loosened some of the cracks running along the ceiling above me, its original alabaster surface now soured into a musty yellow. I noticed that Pa hadn't closed his door properly; the bolt had fallen off the strike plate of the frame with a piercing clap of metal-on-metal, causing it to drift ever so slightly ajar.

My father's voice soon rumbled from inside his room. He was on the phone with someone. Was he talking to Mum? I left the sofa and crept up to his door in about three seconds. I waited there, holding my breath, listening to him speak.

He *was* indeed on the phone with my mother. Having a conversation that would end up lasting the grand total of a minute. I strained my ear, but couldn't really make out much of it from outside the room. Not that it mattered anyway; I already knew she wouldn't be coming home for the funeral.

Why couldn't Pa have given me the phone, even for a few measly moments? Mum had been gone six months and I'd not heard her voice since the day she had left. And it wasn't like everyone else had been missing out; whenever she had called this house, Pa had managed to hog the vast majority of her calls, and

I'd missed out on the rest due to some horrendous twists of fate, like the time she had called while I was out on a class trip, or that evening I had got locked outside the house and the doorbell had stopped working too.

I was badly due a chance to speak to Mum. Pa owed it to me. It was getting to the point where every time I heard any phone ring, the first thought that would pop into my head was, "Is it her? It just might be her this time."

My father was now mumbling to himself angrily. Pa always got angrier when he called Mum, and this time was no exception; he had practically slammed the phone back in its place when the call had ended. I listened in on my father's mutterings, hoping to catch any information I could from it; I thought I heard him say "Dubai", but I wasn't sure if I had heard right. Was Mum going to Dubai? It couldn't be.

I peeped into the room through the crack left open by the door, and I saw him, shoulders heaving visibly, reach back for the phone and dial again. He was slumped on the edge of his queen-sized double bed, his feet resting on the lower shelf of the mantelpiece that held the telephone and a directory. The rest of the room was bare and without furniture, save for the small TV set that was placed in one corner. It was the biggest room in our house, but it looked more like a spare one that no-one used, and the closest thing in it that came to a decoration of some sort was the swirly design of the iron grilles that barred the exterior of each window.

Ultimately, I decided to slip in, already sure that he was going to scold me for it. I hadn't asked his permission to enter, but I had to find out what had gone on between him and Mum."Your *Ah Kong* is gone," he said simply, putting the phone down. His tone was surprisingly even.

"I know. *Ah Peh* called and told me. Is Mum coming home for the funeral?"

Pa's face had the same look it had from the time I had asked him about the meaning of the word "copulation" (thanks to some brilliant advice from my oh-so trustworthy friends).

"No. And your brother isn't answering his phone."

"You actually called him?"

Pa had kicked Michael out of the house two and a half months ago, after my brother, hard-pressed to scrounge up sufficient cash for a used motorcycle on a cut-price offer, decided to be very enterprising with a few of Pa's prized possessions. It was something that we'd all seen coming for a while. My sixteen-year-old brother had a history of acting up, but after Mum had left, he went totally out of control. I'd not seen or spoken to Michael since, and as far as I knew, nobody knew where he was; not even Pa. But I didn't worry so much about him. He was a dumbass, and his only purpose in life seemed to be making life difficult for everyone else in the house. Besides, it seemed like he was probably tough enough to last out there on his own, like a cockroach surviving a nuclear blast. A giant, six-foot-tall, annoying cockroach. I was sure he was happier wherever he was.

"Start packing," Pa said. "I'm going to pick up Jen and Aaron now. Then, we're leaving for your *Ah Peh*'s house."

"Today? But what about school?"

"I've called the school. You're all going to be away for two days."

"Oh." I couldn't resist myself. I had to ask him about Mum. "Did I hear something about Mum going to Dubai?"

"What did you hear?" His tone was still steady, but his eyes were growing darker, and his slightly protuberant jaw, which had been inherited by all his offspring, was suddenly clenched and trembled visibly. "You were eavesdropping on me, weren't you? I thought I've told you many times not to do that."

"I was just … I wanted to find out about Mum. Maybe speak to her a bit …"

"Well, you can forget about that for a while. She is going to Dubai tomorrow. And she says she won't be able to call us from there."

"How long will she be there?"

"I don't know for how long. As long as the doctors say she needs. Why don't you send her an e-mail and ask her yourself?"

Mum being unwell was the lie Pa told everyone, and it was also the reason Mum herself had given us for leaving home. They had both given us the excuse of an unspecified malady that could only be treated across the seas and down under. I knew this wasn't the truth though. Mum had been the healthiest person in all Brunei, or at least our household, and I'd never seen her ill before. Not one sniffle or cough, even when the rest of us were hacking and snorting and flinging our snot everywhere. However, I also knew that, especially around the time of her leaving home, the healthiest person I had ever known, and the person least likely to ever need the services of a doctor in Brunei, let alone one overseas, had been the unhappiest as well.

We kids usually e-mailed her a few times a week, but so far, we'd only received a handful of replies from Mum. The most recent one was a five-line paragraph she had sent us a month ago, addressed to Jen and talking about the Australian weather and about a wonderful *dim sum* place she had found in Melbourne.

"I … Maybe we could call her one more time then. Before

she leaves."

"Stop nagging me, Jonathan! And we have no time to do that. We've got to leave for your *Ah Kong*'s funeral soon. Let her call us when she wants to."

Pa pursed his lips to show he was done talking about this. He handed me a plastic bag full of clothes, then followed through with a set of instructions about the funeral gear he'd rented from the temple on the way home. Uncomplainingly, I took the bag back to my room and laid out its contents on my bed: three sets of dark blue shirts and equally dark blue trousers that would serve as mourning outfits for me and Jen and Aaron, in good old traditional Bruneian-Chinese fashion.

I shared the room with Aaron, our two single beds occupying the opposite sides of the small rectangular space that also managed to fit in a cupboard packed to the brim with our books (mostly mine), a wardrobe, two working desks and a dressing table next to each of our beds. It was the second-largest room on the upper floor after Pa's, and was connected to a common bathroom that opened on the other side into our sister Jen's room. And like Pa's, it was also pretty bereft of colour or decorations. Well, there was stuff on the walls, but I'd hardly have considered the posters displaying nauseating platitudes – "Never put off tomorrow what can be done today" or "Time and tide waits for no man" – that my father had us endure as the sort of things a normal kid my age would want in his room. Jeez, those slogans were tiresome even for Aaron.

I dumped all our funeral clothes into my tattered rucksack, which, with its three broken zips and a coin-sized hole at the bottom, was always threatening to give way any minute. Then I moved on to pack myself the other essentials I needed for *Ah*

Kong's funeral. So naturally, in went a couple of choice comics. I knew very well that any family gathering that was not a kid's birthday tended to be mind-numbingly boring, and this one would probably take the cake in that respect. I would surely need something to read while I was there.

The comics were followed by my bathroom stuff, and then my homework. Thanks to a little bout of diarrhoea, I had missed school the past couple of days, and yet, somehow, everything Class 5D, my class, had been working on in my absence was turning up at my desk, awaiting completion. I picked up the sheets with a groan and stuffed them into my bag. I had two whole practice papers for maths class, and no answers. The only consolation was that Taskmaster Mrs. Yap, our maths teacher, wouldn't be around to see me use my little calculator to help even the odds a bit in my favour.

If there was ever a time when I really needed Mum, it was now. Maths was beginning to get a bit tricky for me, and she was a maths teacher after all. The not-yet-awful but still-noticeable drop in my grades in the recent months was hardly surprising. She wasn't there to teach me at home like she used to. And now she was going to be out of reach for what might as well be forever. It certainly felt that way to me. Maybe if I tried harder, I could persuade Pa into making that one last phone call before she left for Dubai, and before she became more unreachable. I assumed she'd be keen to know how I was getting along and would be happy I had called. Besides, I had so many things to ask her.

Like what Australia was like, and if the people there were all as good looking as they looked on those travel brochures. And if she'd seen a kangaroo yet, and if the steak there really was ten times better than anything we had here, like *Ah Peh* claimed it was. What places she'd visited, and how our Aunt May and her family was doing. And what toys she'd got us ...

And why she had really left. Would she ever come back?

Had life here with us been truly that terrible? It could've been with Pa, but were the rest of us not enough to keep her from leaving? Or was it because of all of us?

Or because of me?

Chapter Two

By the time my father had returned home with Aaron and Jen, I was done packing and was watching TV. We didn't have cable, so I was making do with what was on the terrestrial channels, flipping between an episode of a New Zealand gardening show, which looked suspiciously like something I'd seen last year, and a documentary on camels, or "the ships of the desert" as the show's host liked to call them.

"Aaron," I called out as soon as I heard my eight-year-old brother stomping up the stairs.

"Hey. What's on?" He flopped down onto the chair next to mine, just in time for the afternoon news bulletin. He was still dressed in the white short-sleeved shirt and blue shorts combination that was the standard uniform for most schools in Brunei, including ours. As ever, the pinned-on school badge above his breast pocket was slanted at a distracting, almost 45-degree angle; I had never asked him about it, but I suspected that he was doing it deliberately because he liked the attention it got him from people.

"*... Cases of shoplifting have risen by 50%, police figures have revealed ...*"

Aaron stared at the TV, transfixed by the newsreader's strikingly long, pale and ghostlike face, and the pointed ears that stuck out of his head like little horns. We never could remember his real name, so we called him Daryl, because it kind of sounded like "devil".

"Pa told you, right?" I asked, trying hard to peel my eyes off the TV screen. Had the devil-newsreader grown a tiny beard too? Those ears were really looking awfully horn-like all of a sudden.

"*... as well as congregating in places of ill-repute, such as pool parlours and karaoke lounges ...*"

"Aaron!"

"Huh?"

"*Ah Kong*. He died. You know that, right?"

"Yeah. Pa told me already."

I shook my head at my brother's cluelessness. He was still staring at Daryl instead of concentrating on the important event going on in our lives.

Aaron and I looked a lot like our father, right from our crew-cut hairstyles and deep-seated eyes and large upturned noses, to our lanky frames and flat-footedness. A frequent joke between the two of us brothers was to propose swapping our larger, wider eyes with our sister's considerably narrow pair, if she'd be willing to trade her ideal thin nose with our fatter ones. A fair trade-off indeed if it were possible, we thought, but Jen never quite saw it our way.

In spite of these differences amongst us, the three of us still shared most of our features with our father's side of the family. Only Michael took after Mum's in a significant way. He had a sharper, much more angular face as well as a considerably lower forehead, and his lower jaw stuck out the least amongst us. The resemblance to Mum's side was made complete by his droopy eyes and his considerable height, which was probably the only area in which my eldest brother had ever managed to reach his full potential. Pa was a bit taller than the average Bruneian but Mum was as tall as him, and even then she was by far the shortest in her family.

"... *finding alternative activities for youths to spend time doing, such as playing traditional games like* congkak *and* gasing, *participating in walkathons, attending civic lessons ...*"

"Aaron, he's dead. He's gone. We're not going to see him ever again. Don't you get it?"

"Yes, we will," Aaron snapped, and turned away from the TV to look at me, frowning. Ah, the spell had been broken finally. "We'll see him again in heaven. With all the angels and Kevin's cat, Meemo."

"Cats don't go to heaven, Aaron."

"Yes, they do. The cat angels let them in through the flap on the pearly gate."

"What are you ...? Never mind." I had wasted enough time already. I needed to let him in on what I knew about Mum. Maybe he'd be of some use in helping change Pa's mind. Maybe Aaron could convince him to try calling our mother once again.

"Hey, Aaron, guess what ..." I lowered my voice to a whisper. "Pa said Mum might be going to Dubai very soon." I then added, "For more treatment."

"Oh. From Australia? Straight to India?"

"No, dimwit, Dubai's in Saudi Arabia! Anyway, he said she'll be completely unreachable once she gets there. Not like she was keeping in touch with us too often to begin with, but we really need to talk to her before she goes off again. We could ask her if she wants to visit home sometime. At least come for the funeral. What do you think?"

Aaron shrugged at me. He didn't seem as interested in the

idea. His nonchalance regarding Mum wasn't without reason: Aaron had been near-hysterical around the time she had left, but he had been consoled by my promise that Mum would be gone only for a short time and would return with a lot of presents for him. After that, Aaron took her absence quite easily, and was only optimistic and eager with regard to the bags of gifts that our mother would bring back for him.

I wanted to try coaxing him one more time but before Aaron and I could finish our conversation, our sister stormed upstairs.

"What are you two doing still sitting around? Get ready to go! We're leaving soon!" she ordered, switching off the TV and chasing us into our rooms. Jen reminded me of the sister in *Great Expectations*, but she didn't find the comparison too favourable of course.

Within ten minutes, we had gathered in the living room, ready to leave. Our fourteen-year-old elder sister had done the packing for herself as well as for Aaron, and she now knelt by the front door, fishing out all the extra junk he'd snuck into his bag after she'd thought her work was done. Instead of howling with protest, like I would have if I were in his shoes, Aaron stood there and watched her work, nodding shamefully as our sister scolded him.

"Wuss," I sneered, and Aaron glared at me.

In keeping with the most recent seating arrangement for the car, Jen rode shotgun, leaving my younger brother and me to take the backseat. We pulled out of the driveway in a sombre crawl, leaving behind our home temporarily untended for a few days. Our housekeeper Rosita had left soon after Mum had, and Pa never seemed interested in finding a replacement. He was happy to make do with the weekly visits paid by one of his brother's servants, as well as by Sammy, the odd-job worker who cut our lawn and did a spot of gardening now and then. I did see Pa occasionally trudge around our compound with a hose in hand, but suspected that was more out of the need to take a walk than any genuine concern for the state of our lawn.

Surrounding our modestly sized house, we had grounds spanning about a fifth of an acre. It was a reasonable amount of space, Pa often said. I spent most of my time outside the house on a bike, riding in circles along our driveway rather than playing in the grass, where red ants and stray dog poo were constant dangers. And grass was almost all there was to our garden; it didn't have any plants or flowers, save for the odd mango tree. This was something that Mum had always complained about, that our garden was bare and lacked character. I remember her and Pa having arguments about it, where she would suggest going down to the flower shop in Rimba but he'd always respond that it was a waste of money and effort. Which was ironic because if *Ah Peh* or his wife mentioned our lacklustre garden to him when Mum wasn't around, he would blame her for not having any interest in tending to it.

The ceremony was to be held at my uncle's house, which was also the centre of our little extended family, and where *Ah Kong* had lived out his later years. It was located in Kampung Sungai Beruk, the "village of the river of apes". Well, better than a river of piss, at least. There was a lot of jungle around there, but strangely no discernible river, and I'd not seen many monkeys in the trees behind the house either, so I often wondered where the name could have come from. I could have said the same for many other places in Brunei actually; names here tend to have rather random meanings.

Pa drove in silence, those horrendous sunglasses still perched on his nose. He had chosen to play his favourite CD again, a collection of sappy and slow love songs, the kind that I usually got to hear on life-insurance adverts. As a countermeasure, Jen had plugged herself into her iPod and was probably listening to the hottest Korean idols belt out their tunes. Aaron and I had no such devices of our own, so we would have to make up our own distractions for the drive to the wake.

"So what were you saying about Mum," Aaron began, sounding as bored as I was feeling, but I stopped him from saying anything more. I did want to talk to him about Mum, but not where Pa could easily hear us. Our father definitely wouldn't approve of this choice of topic.

"Let's do this later," I whispered to him. I gestured with my eyes at Pa and shook my head vehemently. Aaron seemed to get the message. He fished out a storybook from his bag and buried his face in it.

The day's copy of the *Brunei Times* lay between Aaron and me, and I picked it up. Here was something: Pa often encouraged us to read newspapers over the so-called rubbish books and comics we liked and he had to buy for us. Under the blue-striped logo of the paper was the front-page headline: "Flood in Tutong expected to worsen." This was accompanied by an aerial image of a district submerged in floodwaters; a second photo showed a gathering of people attempting to bail out a car stalled on the flooded road. The water came up to their waists.

"Look at this news article," I announced to my brother, making sure my father could hear me. "The flood in Tutong is getting worse. This is what happens to the weather when people drive too many cars and don't recycle ..."

“How does that cause flooding?” Aaron asked, putting down his storybook and peering at the newspaper. His eyes however veered towards another story: “Minister opens Chocolate Convention.”

“Well, because, all the carbon dioxide from the fuel we use goes into the air and makes the world hotter.”

“How?”

“Uh, all the hot air can’t escape because the carbon dioxide keeps it in.”

“Yeah.”

“And … Because it gets hotter, more water evaporates, since water evaporates faster when it’s hot.” I paused to catch my breath. “So … we get more clouds, and so it rains more. Yeah, that’s it!”

Hopefully Pa was listening to all this junior scientist stuff I was coming up with. It was going to be hard to keep this going, and any more would get Aaron really started with his questions, especially about the recycling bit. How the hell should I know how recycling helped the weather? All I knew was it was good for the environment.

Having struggled with a science topic, I decided to move on to another. A big map of Brunei took up half the second page, forecasting the weather in the four districts, from west to east: Belait, the oil district; Tutong, the one in the middle and currently flooded; Brunei-Muara, home of the capital, Bandar Seri Begawan; and Temburong, made up of mostly untouched jungle and nature reserves. We lived in the largely residential Berakas area, in the eastern part of the Brunei-Muara district, where it was not expected to rain tomorrow. *Ah Peh* lived about half an hour’s drive further east, close to the port town of (surprise, surprise)

Muara, where it was also not expected to rain tomorrow. The rest of the country wouldn't be so lucky though ... By the looks of the forecast, they'd better forget about sandbagging their homes and focus instead on building arks.

I moved on to a story on the second page that seemed rather interesting: "New shopping venue opens in Kampung Selamat." That was our village, and we were driving through it now, I informed Aaron excitedly as I showed him the article. We were on the main Muara Road that would take us straight towards Muara town in the direction we were headed, or to the capital if we went the other way.

We looked out our windows in the hope of spotting this "new shopping venue". We saw nothing new for a while. There was the gas station that Pa used a lot; it was the only place in the country that didn't have attendants to pump the petrol for you. There was the small post office that was shaped like a triangle, where Jen collected the Japanese and Korean celebrity magazines she ordered online every other week. There were the rows of assorted unfenced single houses, mostly wooden and painted in yellow or blue, nearly all of them showing off at least two to three cars and often an extra motorcycle parked in their respective lots. Interspersed amongst this jumble of homes and vehicles were countless trees, mostly of the palm and coconut variety. Almost all were heavy with ripening or ripened fruit, but it seemed like no-one was bothered about harvesting them, as evidenced by the husks of the many drupes that had gone untouched and lay strewn on the ground. And then I saw it, the shopping centre that the newspaper told us about. It was a two-level concrete building that had embedded within it a minimart and a *dhobi* launderette. I caught it in the nick of time, before we flew past it completely, lodged as it was between all the trees and houses that took up so much of the view.

"That's the new shopping venue I just read about in the newspaper," I pointed out to Aaron, again with my voice raised so Pa could hear. My brother nodded in acknowledgement. I went on to the next article, one on new traffic laws in Brunei, but realised that I was starting to feel a bit nauseous.

We soon emerged out of Kampung Selamat and into Kampung Batu Empat, where the road narrowed down to a single carriageway and was lined with groups of empty, unsold, decade-old houses sitting on foundations as weak as pudding.

"A demerit of at least two points for traffic code violations," I read out loud, wanting with all my heart to tear myself away from the newspaper before it made me puke. I peeked at Pa to see if he was paying attention to me. He wasn't. Aaron had also gone back to his storybook. But I was truly determined to finish this task, and turned the page just as Pa overtook the car in front of us, narrowly avoiding an oncoming truck.

"ASEAN ministers meet in …" I felt suddenly dizzy, "multilateral trade forum …" Oh, this was unbearable. My head was swimming with images of flooded roads and shopping centres and boring dignitaries when I finally shut the paper and threw it aside. My nausea had reached the point where any tiny motion could shake my whole world off balance, so I leaned back in my seat and tried to keep as still as possible. Shutting my eyes, I tried to ignore the sensation that was taking over my body, of being spun around and around on one of those fairground teacup rides. Stupid travel sickness. Why did it have to be me to be the only one to get it from Mum?

I brought a hand up to pinch my nose's bridge. It was a trick I had learnt from Mum, and it seemed to help with the nausea a bit. The act made me briefly remember how she'd do it for me when I was younger, but that image came and went in a flash, and then I was back again on my own, in the present. When I was feeling a little better, I opened my eyes slightly, and through my fingers, I saw that the road and its landmarks seemed very familiar. We were almost there.

Kampung Bukit Seri was the last village before our destination. It lay centred around a hill that at one point was the biggest in the whole Muara area. It was ten years since it had been levelled to make way for housing developments, but any positive results from the hill's destruction still remained to be seen.

"Is this is the place where *Ah Peh* met a ghost?" I found myself asking Pa, out of nowhere.

"There's no such thing as ghosts," he mumbled.

"Did he really …"

"Quiet. I'm concentrating."

This area was apparently known for its spooky happenings. Dense jungle enveloped the houses in the area, and it was here that people said all the spirits lived. Angry that their home had been razed to make way for people, they had sought revenge by haunting the villagers who had occupied their land.

The tales I had heard were of families going to bed one night, and then waking up in the wee hours of the morning outside their houses with no recollection of how they had got there, and of shadowy beings drifting along the roadside and stalking nervous late-night drivers. I found those more convincing than *Ah Peh*'s story: he had claimed that the ghosts had damaged his car's suspension when he had sped through the area (also notorious for its many speed bumps) in a rush to catch the kickoff of a football match. His proof was that he had seen a single, conspicuous-looking leaf in the middle of his lane immediately after it had happened, so obviously the ghost must have transformed into it before it could be seen, and there was no way it possibly could have fallen from the hundreds of trees flanking the entire length of the road as it ran through the village.

The road curved around the hill's base and led to a small hamlet of homes and small stores, and amongst them was a makeshift hut made out of zinc sheets, almost certainly the home of the labourers who were working on the only construction site in the area. Next to this hut was a palm tree that extended far above the earth, looking like a long and tattered umbrella, its leaves fanning out thinly at the top. It was like a scene from a cartoon, the tree and the hut standing there together, little and large, side-by-side, like a pair of old friends, and I couldn't help smiling at it. I pointed them out to Aaron, and he smiled too.

After a few more minutes, the car made a left turn and went up a small slope, on top of which was a landing of sorts that bore a cluster of houses, all linked to a main in-road and fancier than any house we'd seen on the way here. Our destination was the large orange-coloured house at the very end of the road.

Like my grandparents, most of the others in the neighbourhood were old folk, many of them second-generation Chinese who'd settled down here all the way back in the 1920s and 1930s when their migrant parents had laid down the stepping stones. My father and his siblings had grown up with these neighbours and knew them all like they were family; they knew their quirks and nicknames and funny anecdotes and all their relatives.

Standing just beside *Ah Peh*'s house was the house of the patriarch of the Chow family, who were associated with ours through the marriage of one of their daughters with the brother of my late grandfather. Well into his nineties, Mr. Chow lived with his divorced second-eldest son, who worked as a dentist. Nicknamed *Laba* or "spider" (courtesy of a large mole on his forehead with eight spindly hairs projecting from it), the retired shopkeeper was, by all accounts, still quite agile and a regular sight in nearby Muara town, sitting in his usual seat at the coffee-shop and asking anyone who walked by for a cigarette or spare change.

Opposite the lair of the one with the tarantulous birthmark was the home of a distant relative of my grandmother's brother-in-law. The man was called *Kepala besi* or "metal head", and though I didn't know the story behind the name, I had indeed observed the curious anvil shape of his head on the few occasions I had met him. He and his family were among the leading patrons of Brunei's underground gambling dens; however, so many others could make a case for that title in this country that it was hardly a big deal.

Our car entered the compound of *Ah Peh*'s house, which was the largest in the area, although considered fairly average by Bruneian standards; the house was three-and-half-thousand-square-foot big, as our uncle often reminded us, and had grounds that spanned about a third of an acre. *Ah Peh* had certainly left no stone unturned to show the world he was rich. There was a curved satellite dish perched atop the roof. Huge pink plastic flamingos were stationed on the house's neatly trimmed lawns, which came complete with a koi pond and gazebo. And as if to compensate for our lack of decorative flora, our uncle's garden teemed with almost double the amount of flowers and fruit trees that a property this size ought to have had on display. The place looked so packed that the addition of even one more hydrangea would have probably caused it to burst, sending all the plants and trees and prize fish spilling out in an avalanche of excess.

A balcony overlooked the front porch, over which a white banner containing a stream of Chinese characters was now hung. The crimson roof, the colour of fresh salmon, lay flattened over the top of the house like a lid clamped over a shoebox, its paintjob completed over a year ago but still looking sickeningly bright and fresh. It seemed like we were the first ones to make it to the wake; apart from the banner, there was no obvious sign that a funeral would be taking place here soon. I looked around to confirm my suspicions, and saw that the only other cars in sight were the ones belonging to my uncle.

"Okay, let's go in and pay our respects to *Ah Kong*," commanded my father. We waited as he took a few deep breaths to prepare himself. When Pa finally found the will to leave the car, we followed him hesitantly, me dragging my feet and wondering with growing apprehension about what lay ahead of us for the next few days.

"Hey, Jen. You went to Pa's grandmother's funeral last year. What was it like?" I asked my sister as we trudged along.

"I don't know ... Nothing much happened," she shrugged. "Why, are you scared?" That would have normally come out sounding like a tease, but I could hear genuine concern in her voice this time.

"No, I'm not scared." I was sort of scared. This was the first funeral I was attending after all.

It almost went without saying that this would be the first dead body I'd be seeing too. The thought of that alone felt like an invisible force attempting to keep me from moving any closer to the house. I told myself not to be afraid. After all, I knew very well that bad things didn't happen to people just because they went near dead bodies. And that dead bodies couldn't really hurt anyone. It wasn't like *Ah Kong* was going to jump out of his coffin and attack us for brain food, as if we were in some zombie movie.

Or was he? That last movie I had seen at Radzi's house had been unnervingly realistic. Radzi had even told me that it was based on a true story. Perhaps it was best to be careful and keep myself as far away from the body as possible, at least until I was sure it was safe to approach it.

My upper body suddenly made an involuntary shudder. I looked around to see if anyone else had noticed it. They had not. Wrapping my arms around myself, I shuffled towards the others, pushing away thoughts of making an about-face back to the car, while also trying to keep the last vestiges of my travel sickness from rising up once again and spilling out onto the floor.

Chapter Three

The panes of the glass door trembled as we crossed over. My father came to a halt a few steps into the house, as soon as he saw *Ah Kong*.

My grandfather lay on a platform draped in white silk in the middle of my uncle's living room. At his feet were an altar bearing a black-and-white framed photograph, an urn holding the remains of many burnt-out joss sticks, and a tray proffering a selection of his favourite foods and spirits. On the floor beside my grandfather lay a metal basin containing a burning circle of folded paper pieces, placed atop a mound of ash. *Ah Peh* was crouched over it, adding new pieces to the front of the paper-chain as the fire worked its way forwards, and making sure that it kept going on and on in endless circles.

It was going to take me some convincing that this thing in front of me used to be my grandfather. From where I was, it seemed as if a mannequin or a wax dummy, lifeless and pale, had been laid out on the platform. Was that really *Ah Kong*? Sure, it resembled him, but something was very … very "off" about it. Something that wouldn't let me believe that what I was seeing was real. On the other hand, the photograph of him on the altar was a lot closer to how he had looked when he had been alive. But it was only a black-and-white shot, and probably one that had been taken from around the time I was born.

As we walked in, I couldn't help wondering about the necessity for this grand funeral. Considering that my grandfather was no longer living, and had no way of knowing or seeing what was happening here, why did we have to stage this elaborate ceremony around his body? I looked to Pa, ready with the question, but then bottled it away, realising that he wouldn't be too amused by my questions now.

Well, if there had to be a ceremony, *Ah Kong* was certainly dressed for it. His corpse was draped in a fine black suit and trouser set and had been fitted with a pair of Italian shoes; I could tell because the soles were emblazoned with the words "Armany" and "Definitely Made in Italy".

I looked around my uncle's living room, taking in the changes that had been made for the funeral. The spacious hall, twice the size of ours, just as the house was, had once boasted of not one but three coffee tables, each accompanied by its own circle of settees and armchairs, yet leaving enough room for a piano, multiple cabinets, and side tables that displayed photos of *Ah Peh* with various businessmen and government bigwigs as well as his daughter's numerous music awards, not to mention the countless bone-china ornaments that we kids were absolutely forbidden from touching.

The living room's current state was unrecognisable; it had been extensively rearranged to accommodate the platform, where *Ah Kong* lay, and the space around it, where *Ah Peh* was sat, thus confining the common seating area into a small and tight space. And gone were the ornaments, the pictures and the artwork, including the knock-off Mona Lisa that *Ah Peh* especially liked to show off to me.

My uncle greeted us from the floor. He was a slightly larger replica of my father, but with less hair and a very prominent set of buck-teeth.

"Seng," he said flatly, setting his overwrought, cavernous eyes on us .

"Hello, *Ah Peh*," we recited in unison.

"Go pay respect to your *Ah Kong*," he instructed.

Pa had already started on the joss sticks. Aaron bit his lip eagerly, hoping to use the matchbox, but he could dream on. I was still not allowed to light matches, and my little brother was mistaken if he thought he could jump the queue for that privilege.

We collected the smouldering sticks from our father, a pair for each of us, and got in line behind him. Pa stood in front of my grandfather and held out his two sticks with both hands, moving them up and down in prayer slowly. The incense that emanated from their glowing tips tickled my nose and throat, prompting me to hold my own joss sticks as far away from myself as possible. I looked up, following the smoke as it wafted up to the ceiling, and saw that it was making a conspicuous dark stain above the altar.

Once Pa was done, it was Jen's turn. She followed his example, but prayed out loud.

"*Ah Kong*, it's Jen ... Uh, I want to say how much I'll ... I'll miss you ..."

I cringed as I listened to her stumble through her speech, sounding unrehearsed and unmistakably saddened by our grandfather's death, but not quite tearful yet.

"Come on, do it properly," I whispered. The suggestion was meant more for my own ears, but was nonetheless picked up by her very sharp pair. She turned around and glared at me but got the hint. She cut her speech short then planted her joss sticks in the urn.

"Wait, Jennifer," my uncle called out just as she was about to walk away. "Come and kiss your *Ah Kong*. The eldest child must do it. And since Michael is not here, you must."

"Wh-what?" Jen exclaimed, none too enthused. She turned to our father for support, but he simply motioned for her to get on with the ritual.

Gingerly, she moved up to the head of the platform. She looked down and put an apprehensive hand on *Ah Kong*'s brow, touching it ever so gently. Then, she began bending over, lowering her upper body with all the pace of a construction crane shifting its dangling, teetering load. Her lips glanced against *Ah Kong*'s pallid skin, and suddenly she was bolt upright. I held my breath, waiting for something horrible to happen, for *Ah Kong* to jump off the platform and attack Jen like a hungry zombie. But nothing happened. Jen simply walked away from our grandfather's body.

I was next in line. I'd never been a fan of praying out loud, so I tried to do it in my head. I drew a blank; no, there was nothing I could think of, offhand, that would fit the moment perfectly. So, with three shakes of my joss sticks, I stepped aside to allow my brother to say or think his piece.

"Seng, is Michael coming?" my uncle asked my father when Aaron was finished. Pa shook his head.

"Ehh ... How can he not come? That boy ... His grandfather loved him so much, and he can't be bothered to turn up for his funeral?"

None of us answered him. Michael's parting of ways with us was still a taboo topic, and Pa seemed reluctant to discuss my brother's absence with *Ah Peh*.

"It's on his shoulders. I've washed my hands of him," he said simply. "Ming isn't here yet?"

Ming was our aunt, who was much younger than her brothers and who worked in a bank in town. She was married but had no children, and she lived almost an hour's drive from this part of Brunei so we never saw her much outside of the usual get-togethers. She didn't tend to give out presents very often to us kids either, so any talk about her never interested me or Aaron. Plus, she had some really strange interests that she never seemed able to stop yammering about. I'd have figured that with all the self-improvement crap she was into, she'd have realised by now that a big step in the right direction would be to actually pay attention to what others felt and shut up for once.

"No, she's still in Singapore. She's arriving tomorrow." *Ah Peh* shifted his attention to Aaron and me. "Why don't you all say hello to your *Ah Ma*? Go on in, to the kitchen ..."

We walked past the living room and through the small hallway that led into the house's dining-area-cum-dry-kitchen. My grandmother was sitting there in her wheelchair, and beside her was my uncle's wife, Vivian.

"Hello, *Ah Ma*. Hello, *Ah Em*," Aaron and I said in chorus.

Ah Ma looked vacantly in our direction and said nothing. She hadn't said much in the years since her stroke. *Ah Em*, who normally left the grandma-tending to her servant, was currently pressed so close against the older woman that a significant portion of her body was in the wheelchair as well, her ample arm engulfing *Ah Ma*'s shoulders, her fluffy bouffant hair and a tear-stained cheek squished tightly against my grandmother's crinkled forehead. The tears were making *Ah Em*'s ultra-thick mascara and face powder run like poster paint, and some of it was even smudged into her lipstick.

"Oh, you boys, come over here!" cried *Ah Em*. She grabbed

Aaron into a crushing embrace then planted a sloppy kiss on his forehead while he struggled to free himself.

"Your poor, poor grandfather," she cooed, releasing Aaron and imploring me to come into her arms. I held my ground, shifting my gaze from those fat death-traps to my brother, who was in the process of vigorously wiping her lipstick off his forehead.

Ah Em's considerable height (she stood just a bit taller than her husband) was evident even while she was sitting. When she got up, she loomed over *Ah Ma*, her formidable hairdo framing her face like a lion's mane.

"And you poor, poor children! Your mother couldn't come back, could she? Oh dear ..."

I was relieved that she had given up on hugging me.

"Mum is still not well enough," I answered.

"And what about Michael? Why isn't he here?"

"He's not coming. Let it be on his conscience," I repeated my father's words.

"What?"

"Er, well, that's what my father said anyway," I added sheepishly.

Ah Em turned to *Ah Ma*. "*Ah Ma. Le tia, boh? Ah Seng geh kia* ..." she said to our grandmother, each gentle syllable accompanied by soft nudges that nonetheless managed to send *Ah Ma* swaying in her chair like a puppet dangling from strings. It was sad to see her like this. I didn't remember too much of what she had been like when she still had her marbles, but I could recollect images of a kindly, soft spoken woman, sometimes with a cigarette in hand, watching over a much younger me as I played in the garden. I could even remember writing an essay about her when I was six, and had ended up reading it out loud in the school annual show; it had included gems such as "My grandma is very old and she eats many pills everyday to stay healthy". The whole thing had come up to only a few sentences, and it hadn't made much sense either, but I must have liked her enough to have done it in the first place.

"Can she hear you?" I blurted out.

"Oh, she can hear, Jonathan!" *Ah Em* nodded. "She's very sad. It's so very sad ..."

She was snorting into a crumpled tissue when Pa and Jen walked into the kitchen. They seemed unmoved by *Ah Em*'s theatrics.

"You three. Go up and put your bags away," our father instructed.

"Yes, children, go upstairs ..." *Ah Em* made a show of composing herself. "Jen, you can sleep in Frida's room. Jonathan and Aaron, in Kevin's room. Go on up. They're waiting for you."

"They're so brave. It's their third loss this year ..." I overheard *Ah Em* sniffle to Pa on our way out. She never could resist saying this line, or any one of its many variants, every time she saw us. And she always said it when we were leaving a room or were just out of sight but still within earshot, as if she wanted us to hear it but think that she didn't know that we had overheard her. I used to find it weird but now I simply disregarded it, much like I did anything she had to say.

Kevin was upstairs in the play area, again twice the size of the one in my house. He was where he could usually be found, lounging on the couch and reading a comic. The 60" TV in front of him was on, as was the PC placed beside the broken snooker table, which had been re-engineered into a fully-functional, and fully occupied, Lego display. The room's air was frosty, thanks to the air-conditioner being set to full blast.

My guess was that he'd got bored of channel surfing a while ago; the television was playing BBC World, an unlikely choice for my brain-dead nine-year-old cousin.

"That's terrible, isn't it?" I remarked, flopping onto the chair next to his. Aaron remained standing, seemingly more interested in watching the two of us than the TV.

"What're they tearing all those trees down for?" I said, pointing to the television screen. The show was on Peruvian natives losing their homes to loggers.

My cousin shrugged absentmindedly, his pudgy, bowlcut-haired head still stuck in his comic. He stuck a hand into a packet of corn chips that lay beside him and shoved a few pieces into his mouth. Crumbs spilled onto his upper lip and nose as he devoured them, his upturned nostrils twitching with each bite. Mouth still half full, his face suddenly turned into a frown. His hand then shot back into the bag and began rummaging around.

"I thought there was supposed to be a toy in here ..." he moaned. I gave him an impatient sigh and gestured to my bag.

"Oh right ..." Kevin finally realised what he was supposed to do and set his comic and bag of chips aside. He licked his fingers clean and got up. "Want to put your stuff in?"

"Yeah, thanks," I answered, and my brother and I followed him into his room.

Kevin's room was what our dreams were made of, down to the tiniest detail. He had a massive study table, a swivel chair, two cupboards crammed with *manga*, a laptop, a water bazooka, a toy display shelf, pool cues, a dartboard, a blackboard, a whiteboard, a kickboard, and about a million board games, most of them stacked in a pile in a corner, still unopened. As always, I was unable to peel myself away from all his incredible stuff, staring around the room and feeling a mixture of breathless wonder and bitter envy.

"Just drop your bag there."

I left my rucksack propped up against one of the cupboards, while Kevin plopped himself onto his chair and gave himself a little twist. The sight of his rotund form twirling atop the slender leg of the chair almost made me crack up. If only he had on a blue and green shirt, then he would have made for a spitting image of a spinning globe.

"So, *Ah Kong*'s gone ..." I said, composing myself.

"Yeah, I know." Kevin flipped through the exercise books on his desk absentmindedly.

"How's *Ah Ma*?"

He shrugged. "You saw her downstairs, didn't you?"

"Right ... What about your father?"

Kevin didn't answer. Instead, he made eyes at my rucksack.

"What games did you bring along?"

"I didn't bring any."

"Why not?"

"You've got more games than me. What makes you think I'd have something you don't already have?" I said curtly.

"Kevin, what's that?" Aaron, who'd been a silent observer so far, was heading towards our cousin's bed. On it was a magic talking board, occupying centre stage on the lower half of his bunk bed, lying amidst an army of assorted action figures and toy cars.

"Don't! You can't use it now," Kevin yelled as Aaron reached out to touch the board. "We're having a funeral in the house, you know."

Aaron stared back at us blankly.

"It's used to talk to spirits," I explained.

"Wow! We can use it to talk to *Ah Kong* then! Ask him what heaven is like and all that ... Let's use it now, come on!" Aaron was grinning excitedly.

"No! You can't use it during a funeral. It's not safe!" Kevin repeated then got off his chair. He picked it up and set the board on the top bunk of his bed, away from Aaron, making it clear that my brother wasn't allowed to touch it.

"But I want to try ..." Aaron begged. "Please, Kevin!"

"No. You can't use it."

What was up with Kevin? For someone who'd been rather close to *Ah Kong*, he didn't seem all that keen on using this opportunity to contact our recently deceased grandfather. It was also odd that he wasn't letting Aaron play with his new gadget. Kevin almost never missed a chance to show off his latest toys to us less fortunate cousins.

"Have you played with it before?" I myself was intrigued by the concept of the board.

"You can't use it either!"

"I was just asking."

"Well, obviously I have!"

"Did it work?"

"Uh, sorta ... Look, I'm not going to let you guys play with it now, okay? *Ah Kong*'s body is right there downstairs!"

"Wouldn't that make it easier to talk to him?" I challenged. "His spirit's probably hanging around here somewhere ..."

"No! There are no spirits here!" Kevin insisted. "It's ... uh ... Let's not do it out of respect for him, okay? Besides, playing with it would be just plain dangerous for you two anyway. You have weaker *chi* than me and might get taken away by them."

"The spirits can take you away?" Aaron sounded spooked.

"No, they can't," I scoffed. "He's just talking rubbish."

"Oh yeah? What about Peter Poo 'Pants'? He and Mos came over a few weeks ago. A spirit called John Major wanted Pants to reveal the password to his e-mail account, and when he said no, the spirit used its powers to make him shit himself. Right where you're standing."

I immediately leaped a good metre or so to the side. "Eww! Why didn't you tell me?"

"Relax, it was cleaned up. But he shit so much that he almost died and got taken away by the spirits. So that's the true power of the board, if you're not strong enough to resist it."

"Really?" I was skeptical. "But it was Peter Poo. Since when doesn't he shit himself anywhere but the toilet?"

"This was different. I told you, he shit so much that he almost passed out. Mos definitely fainted from the smell. Oh, there was so much on the floor and on his clothes ..."

"Alright, enough!" I yelled.

"I don't want to play with it anymore ..." Aaron mumbled. Guess that story changed his mind.

"That makes two of us," I agreed, before trying to change the subject. "So, how're we sleeping tonight?"

After a heated discussion, the three of us came up with an arrangement that had Aaron taking the floor and me taking the bottom bunk of the bed. We then headed downstairs for dinner. We were to assemble at the same table where *Ah Ma* and *Ah Em* had been sitting at earlier on, and in accordance with our family's custom, we kids were going to have our dinner before the adults.

Jen and Frida, Kevin's sister, were already seated there when we arrived. Frida smiled faintly at us as we sat down, with just the right amount of polite acknowledgement. While not the best of friends, Jen got along with Frida better than she did a lot of other people. It probably helped that our families never pitted the two of them against one another, in the way our parents often compared school results between Kevin and me. Of course, that was probably because, in the eyes of *Ah Em* and *Ah Peh,* Jen wasn't even a worthy rival to their daughter.

Unlike the rest of us, Kevin's sister went to an international school, a very reputable institute according to my uncle, and one where she had the opportunity to immerse her overachieving fingers in all kinds of curricular and extra-curricular pies. From what *Ah Peh* had told us, Frida studied hard to maintain the 90% average across all tests and assignments that she had held throughout her first year in secondary school, and she spent her free time learning the violin – she was presently studying the instrument at a grade seven level and all her best friends were from the school's violin club – and writing poems, a few of which had been published in an Australian teen magazine. Frida's busy schedule worked in Kevin's favour though; it wasn't in every household that the little brother got complete control over the household TV, video and game selections.

Also unlike the rest of us grandchildren, Frida was quite good looking. Fortunately for her, she hadn't inherited any of the Lee genes, nor did she have any tendency towards her mother's height and personality traits. Her dainty, delicate features, sizable eyes and slender nose made her the prettiest girl of her year-group, and she was quite a contrast to Jen's rounder, stockier build. Frida also happened to look the most brooding out of us all, and it sort of made her all the more attractive for it. I'd be lying if I denied having had a crush on her up until last year. Those feelings often threatened to spill out even now, but I kept them a secret, much like how I keep it a secret that I still wet the bed every so often. I suspected that Aaron had a crush on her too, but I had never brought this up for discussion with him so far, and certainly never would in the future.

The five of us ate our dinner in silence. We were being served lamb curry, vegetables, sweet-and-sour pork, braised chicken, beef bone soup, noodles, and spring rolls (fried and non-fried) to go with the two types of rice available (white and brown). A fairly typical meal at my uncle's place, and most of it ended up on Kevin's plate, and my cousin devoured his ample helping with a distinct lack of enthusiasm. When we were done, Jen and Frida dashed off upstairs quickly, without as much as a "see you later" to us. It was just us boys again, and this made me feel comfortable enough to try resuming my conversation about Mum with Aaron.

"Aaron, I'm going to try and ask Pa again about Mum," I began. Kevin didn't seem to be paying us any attention. He was finishing off his third bowl of soup while one of his servants cleared the table around him. "I wanted to ask him earlier, but … you know …" I didn't have to explain myself; Aaron knew I had been too scared to ask.

"We need to talk to her by tomorrow. We haven't spoken to her in so long …"

My stomach began to rumble. Oof, was it the diarrhoea trying to make its last hurrah? My tummy never took too kindly to the food at my uncle's. Yeah, there was plenty of it here, but it was nothing compared to Mum's cooking; her food had that special something that I didn't get anywhere else. I thought about the special noodles she made with diced vegetables that were so perfectly crispy, and her thin-cut chicken breast slices wrapped around mozzarella and chopped ham, my favourite. Eating her food always made me feel like I was having a good day, regardless of how terrible it might have really been.

"Not really." Aaron shrugged. "I spoke to her last week."

"What?"

"Yeah, Mum called us last week."

This was unexpected. Why hadn't anyone told me? "When? Why didn't you tell me?"

"It was on Wednesday. Oh, yeah, you were at tuition, that's why. And ... er ... Pa told us ..." Aaron was twisting in his seat uncomfortably. "He told us not to tell you."

"I can't believe this." Why had Pa wanted to hide this from me? My mouth suddenly tasted bitter. "What time did Mum call? I came back at 8.30."

"I think it was right after you left. At 6.00. Around that time."

I was on the verge of exploding. It was Cikgu Zaini who'd pushed the session an hour earlier so he could go visit his sick brother or something. And he didn't even go in the end. That bastard. What I'd give for just one moment alone with his car and a nice, sharp object.

Of course, I knew there was nothing I could do about it anymore. But I was all the more determined now to get what I needed, which was to find a way to talk to Mum before tomorrow.

"Did she say anything about going to Dubai?" I asked as calmly as I could. The wary expression on Aaron's face however told me he'd seen the murder in mine. Kevin could probably see it as well; he had stopped eating and was listening to us quietly.

"No, she didn't. We didn't talk for that long, Jonathan. Maybe ten minutes."

"Did she ask about me?"

Aaron smiled weakly at me. "She said she got us presents. She said they were on the way here in the mail. I think I'm getting that dinosaur book I wanted at the Science Centre ..."

"Screw the dinosaur book! I've got to get Pa to call Mum tonight. I'm getting my damn phone call!"

I stomped off, my head fuming and my stomach gurgling even more. No, I couldn't take a toilet break now. The anger that was drumming up my courage would get flushed away with my shit, and then it would be back to plain old "yes sir" Jonathan again, who wouldn't dare walk up to his father and demand that he get that phone call he wanted.

Pa was still in the hall with my uncle and my grandmother. *Ah Ma* sat slumped in her wheelchair in front of the makeshift altar, staring at *Ah Kong*'s feet, while my father and *Ah Peh* were sat on the floor, tending to the fire in the basin. Around them, their beddings had been arranged in a neat row. Was it for an overnight vigil? Not that I cared about what they were up to. I had other things to worry about.

"Are you all done eating?" *Ah Peh* asked.

"Yeah, we are," piped in Kevin from behind me. Trust him to follow me here in gleeful anticipation of watching me make a scene. I turned and saw that Aaron stood behind me too, looking quite distressed. I sucked in my breath and went for it.

"Pa," I said forcefully. "You didn't tell me about Mum calling home last week."

His fingers froze and stopped with the paper-burning, but he didn't look up to face me. After a few seconds, he continued feeding the fire as though I'd not said anything.

"Pa. I didn't get to talk to her. Can I call her now?"

"Stop it. I told you not to nag me about this, Jonathan." He still wasn't looking at me.

"What's this about, Seng?" *Ah Peh* seemed curious.

"Mum's going to Dubai tomorrow and she said she won't be in touch for a long time." Pa flashed me a dirty look for this. My stomach growled again and so loudly that I was sure everyone in the room had heard it. "I haven't talked to her in so long …"

"Seng, just let him talk to his mother," *Ah Peh* chided my father. "Why doesn't she want to be contacted? Now if it were me, I'd make sure that …"

"I don't want to talk about this now," Pa mumbled, but *Ah Peh* didn't seem to notice.

"She's gone for treatment, you say? Well, I know a few doctors in Dubai. But isn't Dubai very hot? I've been there once before, and it was so hot there that I had to stay in the hotel 90% of the time. It was like trying to walk around in an oven! Mary never did like hot places, did she? Why didn't you ask me for help, Seng? Singapore is so much closer and the doctors there are just as good. Or even better! I have a friend who knows a very good one working on Orchard Road. This doctor has his photo stuck on all the MRTs. I can arrange for Mary to see him in a week."

"She has friends in Dubai. She will be fine there," my father interrupted.

Ah Peh gave him a smirk. "What friends? Are you sure you can trust them?"

"I'm sure." Pa abruptly turned to me. "Jonathan. I'll talk to you about this later."

"But …"

"I said later!" he snapped. "Why don't you go upstairs and get ready for bed now."

I knew the conversation was over. I nodded grudgingly and charged up the staircase, my stomach hammering anxiously. Kevin and my brother didn't follow me this time; they probably wanted to stay on and see what the adults were getting up to.

So much for the fight left in me. And now I was almost certain that Pa would pay me back in kind for embarrassing him in front of his brother. Could *Ah Peh* have conceivably weakened Pa's resolve by even a smidgen so that there was still a chance of getting what I wanted? That I was clinging on to this as a last strand of hope was enough proof of how dire my prospects really were.

Chapter Four

I looked in the mirror as I rubbed my hands together vigorously and built up a mound of Dettol froth around them. The first glimpse of my face startled me. I had no idea I looked or felt that miserable. I forced my lips to curl up into a grin, but the boy in the mirror stared back at me with an eerie sort of crazed glee. And it felt so heavy to keep my lips up, especially the corners, as if physical weights had been tied to them. The strain wearing me down, I allowed my mouth to drop back to its default look, and I was almost relieved that I only looked sullen again, instead of a psycho kid.

I had chosen this bathroom because it was the only one in the house that had a hose next to the toilet seat, and I could use it to wash my behind and make sure I got everything off. Coming upstairs and away from the others in the family had come as a surprisingly welcome break; it was nice getting a couple of minutes of calm to myself, even if it had been spent on the loo.

With my relentless diarrhoea hopefully laid to rest, it was now time to get back to the business of getting that phone call. I opened the door and stepped back into the upstairs common area. The door to Kevin's room was half-open, and I could hear my father's voice coming from inside. I sneaked over to a bookshelf that allowed me a view into the room but at an angle so tight that Pa would've had no chance of seeing me even if he was facing the door. I saw him standing there, turned away from me and looking down at Aaron, who was squatting on the floor, rummaging through some clothes in my bag.

"There you go," Pa said, in an understanding tone that was usually reserved for Jen or Aaron. "Now, tell me again, what you're going to do after you get up tomorrow?"

"I'll brush my teeth, wash my face and put this on," my brother answered.

"Good. You're a big boy now, Aaron. You don't need me or a maid to tell you these things anymore."

"Okay." Aaron dragged my bag across the floor then shoved it in a corner. "Hey, Pa?"

"Yes?"

"Are you going to call Mum for Jonathan? He didn't get to talk to her last week."

Pa sighed deeply. My fingers dug hard into the edge of the shelf as I waited for his answer.

"Your mother needs to rest before she leaves for Dubai. Maybe she'll call again when she reaches there ... Why did you tell him about the call?" Pa asked, lowering his voice. "I told you and Jen not to say anything to him."

That last sentence came like a kick to my gut, and it was a good thing I'd already emptied it a few minutes ago. Pa knew how important speaking to Mum was to me, but he hadn't said anything to me about her call nor had he bothered arranging for me to talk to her on another occasion. He'd just pretended to me like it had never happened, and as usual, my siblings did nothing but mindlessly obey him. I felt foolish for hoping that they'd be of any help.

There's a Malay word called *geram*, and it describes a feeling that no English term I know could properly communicate. Imagine the worst itch in the world, an itch one hundred times worse than the itchiest bite that the itchiest mosquito could ever give you, but that it's inside you, stirring up all your internal organs and agitating them to the point where you're on the verge of clawing and tearing them out with your bare hands if only to make it stop. You can pound the ground with your fists, break things, scream and shout at the top of your lungs ... It doesn't help; nothing helps. That's *geram*. And, like an itch, trying to address it only makes it grow stronger and last longer. Well, that was what I was feeling, to the point where I was physically trembling where I stood, half-ready to charge in and try tackling Pa to the ground, just so I could punch him in that soulless rock-face of his, again and again until I could break it down to expose what was hidden underneath.

Thankfully, the other half of me quickly took over, and I managed to pull myself away from the bookshelf and walk soundlessly past the door and down the stairs, away from my father.

When I saw my uncle and aunt standing around the foot of the staircase, speaking to each other in low voices, I halted, and remained on the landing where the stairs made a 180 degree turn before they climbed down. I was not more than a few metres away from them, but *Ah Peh* and *Ah Em* were deeply engrossed in their conversation and weren't aware of my presence. A good portion of the living room was visible to me, and I saw Jen and Frida sitting near *Ah Kong*'s platform. My sister was carrying on with the paper-burning task that I'd seen *Ah Peh* doing earlier on, and my cousin was busy folding sheets of yellow paper into small boxes and putting them into a sack that was almost full with them.

"I don't understand what the problem is. He should just let the past be and take the poor boy back in. Aaron and Jonathan must be missing him so much," said *Ah Em*.

No, we weren't.

"Seng is too stubborn. Won't let anyone change his mind ... He's always taking the hard way. Remember when he just finished his bond? I said to him, 'Seng, do yourself a favour and come work under me. You'll make at least twice the salary you'd get as a civil servant. You see my big house and my Mercedes? I guarantee you'll be able to buy one for yourself and Mary by the end of the year.' And he just looked at me as if I'd asked him to be my toilet cleaner. He said, 'I was a teacher, so I should stay in education all my life.' There's no helping a man like that."

The tirade left *Ah Peh* wheezing, and *Ah Em* began to brush his brow and caress his arm.

"And don't even get me started with Mary," *Ah Peh* continued, still out of breath. "It's no wonder it all turned out the way it did ... Now I worry about the children."

Oh, really? Wow, thanks for your concern, *Ah Peh*.

"Well, Jen and Jonathan are quite smart. If they went to the same school as Frida, they could be almost as good as her."

Did *Ah Em* really just call me smart? That was something.

"But raising four children all by himself? That's not the way to do it. How long can this go on for? They need someone to look after them, and if Mary isn't going to come back, then for heavens' sake start looking ..."

Ah Peh was probably drunk or high or both if he thought that was seriously going to happen. How I'd laugh about this with Mum the next time we talked. As if Mum would really refuse to come back home. And as if anyone else would be ready to marry a man like my father out of her own free will; chaining oneself to a live volcano might be a less painful experience.

Adults did love to talk about the same old thing again and again, didn't they? I'd overheard this kind of talk before from our relatives after Mum had left, and it was annoying to have to hear it yet again. I wanted to leave; this wasn't worth listening to any further. But here I was in a bit of a tight spot because I didn't want to give away that I'd been eavesdropping on them by climbing down the rest of the stairs, and I didn't feel like going back up either. Or, at least, into Kevin's room where Pa probably still was.

So, back into the toilet I went, and I waited there for another ten minutes until I heard Pa leave.

When I went in, I found that my cousin had joined Aaron in the room.

"That took long," Kevin said with a snide smile. "Have a nice time in the toilet?"

"Did Pa say anything more about calling Mum?" I asked my brother, ignoring Kevin's jibe.

"Huh? How did you know Pa was here?"

"Never mind that. Did he say anything else?"

"Uh, no."

"Okay, did he say anything about trying to find me?"

"No."

"Fine. As long as he isn't after me anymore." It was a small comfort that Pa had forgotten about my earlier indiscretion. "You know, you could have told me about Mum's phone call earlier. Nice timing, Aaron, now that she's leaving again."

"But Pa said ..."

"Can you stop talking about your Mum?" Kevin moaned,

interrupting my brother. "That's all you've been talking about since you've come here. It's boring."

Oh, how I wanted to lay one into his stomach then and there. But then he would go running to the adults and make a big scene of it. Besides, I knew I could never hurt him. He had superhuman flab all over his body, and especially his belly, and it made him indestructible. Like the time he got hit by a car while chasing after a football. Didn't have a scratch on him, but the car got dented so badly the owner apparently had to throw it in the scrap yard.

"Shut up, Kevin."

"Well, I am bored. You're so boring ..."

"Stop being such an ass, Kevin! *Ah Kong*'s just died and I've just found out I might not be able to speak to my mother again for God knows how long. So, yeah, sorry for not being too much fun right now."

Kevin just shrugged. "Well, let's play a dare game then," he said. "Come on, it'll be proper fun."

"Uh ... What?" I had no idea what Kevin was up to.

"A dare game? A dare to do what?" Aaron asked, looking just as confused.

"A dare to ... A dare to go into *Ah Kong*'s room. His ghost is probably still there ... Woooo ..." He made his fingers swim at us, like he was trying to cast a spell, and howled.

"No, Kevin. Stop kidding around," I said.

"I am being serious." He stood up suddenly, back straightened, his belly popping out further. "Besides, this will give us a chance to get some things from his room. It'll be nice to bury *Ah Kong* with some of his stuff. I'm sure he'd like that."

That did kind of make sense. But I knew the adults wouldn't be too thrilled with our plan. Aaron and I looked at each other, unsure of what we should do.

"Or are you guys too scared? Are you two chicken or what?"

"I'm not scared. I've been there before," I said.

"Then, come on. Don't be a spoilsport. Let's go!"

"Yeah, Jonathan, let's go," Aaron joined in.

"What? You too? I don't even know if we're allowed to go in there."

"Chicken! Bock, bock, bock ..." Kevin flapped his arms and made clucking sounds at me.

"Hey! I'm not, okay. Stop it! Fine! I'll go, I'll go ..." I still wasn't sure what sort of game Kevin was playing, but I wasn't going to stand there and let him call me chicken.

It didn't take us long to get to *Ah Kong*'s room, but we all stopped at the closed door, each of us expectantly eyeing the others and wondering who'd crack first. I was a bit surprised when Kevin made the first move, putting his hand on the doorknob without any encouragement from us. He gave it a twist, and the door let out a mechanical groan. The three of us froze as if we had set off a bomb. We looked back nervously for any sign that we'd attracted the attention of the adults; when we were confident that no-one had noticed, we went inside.

Aaron switched on the lights, revealing *Ah Kong*'s small and rather bare room, which seemed to shrink and keep shrinking under the illumination of the circular, white fluorescent ceiling lamp. The smell of camphor mixed with talcum baby powder filled my nostrils, along with a hint of that nasty green herbal soap that my parents forced me to use every time I complained of an itch. But smells aside, all there was of any note in the room were a small table, curtains with plain floral patterns, and a bed stripped bare of linen. Most of *Ah Kong*'s belongings had probably already been moved or thrown away.

"I don't think we'll find anything here," I remarked. A customary search around the room proved me right.

"I guess you're right," Kevin agreed. And then he switched the lights off.

"Kevin, what the hell!" Good thing I was next to him; I immediately reached out and turned the lights back on, the dark coming and going like a shadow passing through the room. I saw that my cousin already had one foot set out the door, and I guessed his plan was to have closed it on us and hold it shut for as long as possible.

"Oh, you're no fun!" Kevin pouted. "I thought you wanted to be closer to *Ah Kong* and talk to his spirit."

"I thought you said this house had no spirits. And what fun? You want to make Aaron cry and get us all in trouble?" I threw a thumb at my brother, who looked a bit disorientated but thankfully wasn't on the verge of creating a scene yet. "You know he's afraid of being in dark rooms. What the hell's wrong with you?"

"Don't yell at me," Kevin's face darkened. "This is my house."

"I don't care," I raised my voice. "You tried to lock us in, you jackass!"

"Guys, stop fighting," Aaron's voice was trembling dangerously, ready to break into cries any moment now.

"No, I didn't. And you're the jackass, Jonathan."

"Shut the hell up, Kevin."

"Yeah, you are a jackass," Kevin spat angrily. "That's why no-one likes you! No-one wants you, and even your mother doesn't want you!"

"Oh, that's so clever. Come on Aaron, let's go …"

"I mean it. She called last week at that particular time because she knew she wouldn't have to talk to you then."

"Oh yeah, Mr. Psychic? I so believe you!" I grabbed Aaron's hand and started to walk away.

"But she talks to Michael though. Because she likes him. Bet you didn't know that."

Now that got my attention. I froze in my tracks. "What are you talking about? Michael's off on his own. He doesn't talk to anyone."

"Just because he doesn't talk to you doesn't mean he doesn't talk to other people," Kevin smirked arrogantly, much like how his father usually did. "We message each other. He told me."

"Why would he message a little butterball like you?"

That got to him alright. Considering all the insults he was dishing out to me, he never could take it if I gave it back to him, especially about his weight.

"I'm not fat!" he cried. "And your Mum isn't coming back! Not ever!"

My eyes flicked to Aaron, who was looking increasingly harrowed. His face reminded me of the time Michael had told us that Santa Claus was evil because his name was an anagram of "Satan". That had given Aaron so many sleepless nights. And guess who had to put up with it all through no fault of his own?

"Shut up, Kevin," I hissed. "He's going to cry."

Kevin wasn't listening. "She told Michael she wasn't coming back, I swear! Your dad is just pretending she will."

"Is that true, Jonathan?" Aaron asked me in a high trembling voice, and his eyes began to well up.

"Uh ... well ..." I knew the right thing to do was to reassure my brother, but I was just as taken aback by Kevin's words;

true or not, they offered some clarity about the Mum-situation, especially compared to the six months of uncertainty I had been facing thus far.

"She's not coming back?" Aaron pressed on. "You said she was ..." He stood there, tears and snot running down his face, and long, drawn-out sobs racking his body.

I was still looking for the right words to comfort Aaron, but couldn't find any. "Look at what you did!" I turned to Kevin instead and caught hold of his collar. "You made him cry, and now they're going to come up and punish the both of us. Thanks to you and your ... your lies!" Finally, I had managed to deny Kevin's claims. But I was a bit too late.

"I'm not a liar! It's not my fault!" Kevin hollered. "He's just a cry-baby, crying all the time!" And then Kevin burst into tears as well, breaking into deafening shrieks that initially sounded like mad laughter to me.

"I didn't make him cry! I didn't lie!" he screamed, hopping about and slapping the wall with his palm. "It's all your fault! Yours!"

I knew this was going to end badly for me. Three kids were in a room, and two of them were crying. Guess which one was going to get blamed?

I heard the sound of footsteps rushing up the stairs, and the next thing I knew Pa and *Ah Peh* had appeared at the doorway behind Kevin. My uncle knelt down beside his son immediately and began consoling him; Pa patted Aaron on the back a few times, then his hand clamped down like a vice on my shoulder, and he half-dragged half-carried me from *Ah Kong*'s room to Kevin's. Inside, he threw me down onto Aaron's unravelled mattress. It didn't cushion my fall too much, and I landed hard on my side.

"What did you do?" Pa demanded, bearing down on me and blocking out my entire field of vision. "What did you say to your brother?"

"I didn't do anything! Kevin made him cry."

"You tell me now or …" He reared his hand up, fingers splayed open and quivering eagerly for a collision with my flesh.

"I told you, I didn't start it! Kevin said that Mum was never coming back, and Aaron …"

"And you both believed him? Did I ever say she was never coming back home?" Pa demanded, breathing heavily into my face. "What were you all doing in your *Ah Kong*'s room in the first place? Have you no respect for your dead grandfather?"

His face was flush with raw anger, and the way he held back his lower lip with his upper one meant that he was past the point of no return. The rage had taken over, and there was nothing I could do now to stop him.

"We were just … Kevin wanted to play a dare game …"

"A dare game? You think you can fool around like this during your grandfather's funeral?" Pa's hand came down so quickly that I realised I had been hit only after my head had snapped all the way to my right. Everything he said after that went straight past me, like I was a shade from beyond this world, out of reach even to Kevin's talking board.

"… So you'd better behave yourself tomorrow. Understand?" Pa was saying when I finally snapped back. I nodded blankly, still in a daze. My face felt hot, and the slap still stung. Pa rose and gave me an odd look, as though he suddenly didn't recognise who I was. He looked at the palm he had used to slap me and, briefly, I almost thought I saw his head turn away from it, like he was flinching from his own hand. When had Pa hit me before? I couldn't really remember … However hard he was on me, getting any sort of physical punishment from him was incredibly rare.

The moment passed, he turned and walked out, leaving me to think about how this was all my fault.

My fault.

It was always my fault.

It wasn't Aaron's fault for being such a cry-baby or Kevin's for being such an asshole. No, everything was always my fault, because I was the one who didn't point the finger first. I was the one who was the slowest to react, the last to get out of the way, the one who tried to stand and reason with a steamroller of a father.

So, of course I deserved it all, didn't I? For being so stupid. For not being smart enough to pin the blame on someone else. I kept falling for the same trap again and again. I never, ever learnt. What an idiot I was. A hopeless weakling.

And then it came. That dreaded feeling. Whatever you do, no matter what else happens, don't you start crying now, I told myself. I wasn't a wuss like Kevin or a cry-baby like Aaron. I wanted to do anything I could to hold it back. Anything! I had to stop myself from crying.

I kicked my bag as hard as I could. I tore open its zip and grabbed at all my clothes and books. I threw them about, sent them flying. Who gave a shit about homework? I stamped on them, crushed them, and then flung them away. Then, I looked around for more things. Nothing left? What about Aaron's stuff? Or Kevin's? I had to find something!

Ah, yes, my watch. A good choice. The one Pa gave me for my birthday last year, the one that cost $100, and the one I polished and cleaned so often I could see my face on its glass cover. There it was again, my wretched, sour face looking just as miserable as it had looked in the bathroom mirror. I suddenly couldn't stand looking at it anymore. This is what you deserve, I declared in my mind, and I tore the watch off my wrist and threw it on the ground.

"I hate you! You jackass, you never do anything right and you never will!" My foot landed solidly on the watch, shattering its glass cover into a thousand pieces. I heard the hands and the gears underneath crunching to the movement of my foot grinding into them, and I dug my heel in more, savouring the sound. When I'd had my fill, I looked down at the massacred time-piece, ready to finally feel a little better.

Instead, all I felt was deep regret. Not so much about wasting the money Pa had spent on the watch, but about destroying the watch itself. It felt as if I had just brutally murdered something that had lived, a thing that had a soul. Like I had with my own face, I couldn't bear to even look at it now. I picked up the watch's remains and disposed of them in my cousin's dustbin.

The rest of my handiwork was strewn all over the floor. I got down on my knees at once and started fixing what I could, putting back my bag and clothes where they had been and straightening out the torn, crumpled up sheets. It was a good thing that I'd not started on my homework at all, for the things that had suffered the most were my blank foolscap pad and my textbook, the former still half-empty and the latter salvageable with bits of scotch tape here and there. Thankfully I hadn't busted anything else, particularly anything else that wasn't mine.

Done with the cleaning up, I crashed on the bed, exhausted. I ended up lying curled up on the lower bunk of the double bed, as pressed up against the wall as I could be – I wished I could stay like this for the rest of my life. Nothing mattered to me anymore. Everybody in the family was against me. Pa didn't like me and he was certainly not going to call Mum for me. And I was never going to see or talk to her again. Besides, she didn't want to talk to me anymore. She liked Michael and Aaron and Jen, and wanted to talk to them. She didn't want me. I should've known all along.

The pillow that my head was resting on started to feel uncomfortable, and I brought a hand up to touch it. It was soaking wet. I realised that tears were streaming down my eyes and onto it in generous gushes; I had been caught totally unawares, that too by my own thoughts.

Rolling over, I went prone and buried my face into the pillow. That would muffle any sounds I might make and hopefully draw my tears out faster, getting me dry as soon as possible. And if I could be lucky for just once today, maybe it would stop me breathing entirely before the others could come back to see me for what I truly was. A coward.

Chapter Five

By the time a drained Aaron and an uneasy Kevin were led back into the room, I had picked myself up and was sitting cross-legged on my bunk, putting up my best nonchalant front and looking busy with my maths homework, the tear-stained pillow conveniently turned over and tucked beneath the duvet. There had been no need to suffocate myself after all; my brother and my cousin had taken far longer than me to recover from the fight and compose themselves.

It was bad enough that I'd resorted to doing homework as a way to get myself through the remainder of the evening. What was worse was how something that was usually painful could turn out to be a calming and relaxing experience; I was positively buzzing on long division and geometry. I reasoned that this was at least partly because I had brought along my good old G2 black pen with me. It was my lucky pen, unbeaten in the pen-flicking games I played on tabletops with my friends, and one of my best buddies for all of five years and still counting. The lovely black ink it produced was always dark and rich, because it was always just wet enough to shine, but not too wet that it smudged over the paper like most fountain pens did.

Black ink was so much stronger, so much bolder than the crappy blue Mrs. Yap preferred. School work required me to write down facts and figures that were important, and irrefutable, as the teachers said they were, and stood as articles of wisdom handed down since the dawn of civilisation from one generation to another, the kind of stuff we had to remember for life. So why wasn't I allowed to use something that made it all look as important as it was? Blue was a weak ink. Black ink on white paper, now that looked like the perfect representation of truth absolute.

Mrs. Yap didn't care for black ink though, and she insisted that we pupils never use it in her class. This only made me love the pen even more, and I wrote with it every chance I got – which meant I used it only occasionally, and whenever I got the impression that she'd forgotten about the last telling-off she'd given me over the pen. She rarely escalated it beyond a yelling, which I accepted as a sort-of unofficial license to use my G2 every so often. The most recent warning I'd received from her had come fairly recently. Maybe a bit too recently, and that was why I'd opted for a blue pen earlier in the day. But that was then and this was now; I was in so much crap already that I no longer cared about what that bitch would say. There was nothing she could do that would make things worse than they already were for me.

My studious turn-of-leaf served to put the adults off any sort of interaction with me for the rest of the night. When *Ah Em* and *Ah Peh* came in to brief us on the next day's events, it was all directed at the other two. All I got was a cursory reminder to wake up on time the next morning, as well as the routine questions about if I had taken a shower and brushed my teeth. Kevin and Aaron didn't speak to me either, but that was to be expected.

After that, the grownups went downstairs to continue with their overnight vigil over *Ah Kong*'s body. The girls were joining them too; they'd been recruited to handle the midnight shift. The only job left for us boys to do was to go to bed.

My roommates did that without a problem, and it left the room library-quiet, with only the gentle hum of the air conditioner playing in the background. The silence didn't prove too helpful in letting me sleep though, and this was despite me being completely spent from all that had happened earlier and then going into a homework-doing frenzy and wiping out a good third of my maths debt. What was wrong with me? I felt so heavy lying on that bed, with barely enough energy to keep myself breathing. Why the hell couldn't I fall asleep?

A rustling noise from above perked my ears. Seconds later, Kevin's face appeared from over the edge of his bunk, upside-down. In the greenish glow of the nightlight, his round head looked like a big, fat gourd.

"Hey, are you awake?" he whispered.

I didn't answer him. I simply lay there, staring straight up at Kevin's mattress and observing how it was being squeezed tightly into the spaces between the bed's wooden boards by his heavy flab.

"Are you still mad?" He slung himself down the bed's stepladder, and his mattress released a squeak of relief as its springs readjusted themselves. He clearly wanted something from me, and I knew that he wouldn't leave me alone until I responded. I wasn't really that upset with him anyway; despite his considerable girth, there were far heavier burdens dragging me down.

I sat up and gave him a questioning nod. In return, he came over and perched on the edge of the lower bunk. Out came his right hand, and it held his brand new smartphone, its bright screen a good enough replacement for the room's main lights. He smiled at me then started flicking through his list of contacts.

"Here, I told you I wasn't lying," he said, handing me the phone. It was indeed a chat thread between him and Michael. "He does message me, Jonathan."

"'Did you see if our dad made Jonathan cry?' … 'I'd have loved to have seen that, ha ha' … 'Did the little toad get punished?'" I read the texts out loud.

"Go back up." A flustered Kevin stuck his finger over the screen and began scrolling up through the messages, so they went backwards in time.

"'I don't measure with a tape because the sides are too sharp'," I read from the screen, and flashed Kevin a curious glance. My cousin winced.

"Don't look at that!" His finger was moving furiously now.

"'You have to delete the cookies as well'," I read aloud again, then grinned at my cousin.

"Gah, further up!" Kevin grimaced.

I was enjoying torturing my cousin, but at the same time, I was feeling a little niggle about my elder brother being in touch with Kevin, and on such friendly terms too. It was almost like … No, I couldn't be jealous. Over Michael?

"'Got to go now; expecting a call from my Mum'." There it was, dated around three weeks ago. "'You talk to your Mum?' … 'Yeah, once in a while' … 'How's she doing?' … 'Alright. She's glad to be out of Brunei'."

And that was it, a mere five messages about Mum before they had talked about whether Kevin was interested in selling Michael any of his old phones for cheap.

Glad to be out of Brunei? Well, she would be glad, wouldn't she? Mum had been in quite a bad way around the time she had left, so I imagined all those months of relaxing and not having to deal with the demands and responsibilities of her old life would've been a welcome break. But that didn't mean she didn't want to come back. Once she was done with her break, she'd be back home and ready to start over afresh.

"Where does it say that she's never coming back?" I demanded from Kevin.

"Oh, it doesn't? Maybe Michael told me that over the phone ..."

"Well, Michael's an idiot. Just because she's getting a good rest doesn't mean she's not going to come home ever."

"I know what he told me. He talks to your Mum quite often and knows what's happening with her. Why don't you ask him yourself?" Kevin grabbed the phone from my hand. "But ... Oh, wait ..." Kevin scrolled down to the latest message my brother had sent him that night; it said not to message Michael anymore on the current number because he was selling it to a friend, and that he would give Kevin his new number once he got one.

"Sorry, you'll just have to wait."

"Wait? But what about Mum? She's leaving for Dubai tomorrow! Michael didn't say anything about that?"

"Er, no ..."

"You two are useless! I need to talk to him now! At this rate I'll have to wait till the end of time to find the truth. Call him up!"

"Okay, okay, maybe he's still using this number. Let me try, okay."

My cousin pressed on Michael's name and put the phone to his ear. Aaron remained asleep on the floor, oblivious to the ruckus we were making. I wondered if I should wake him up, so he could talk to our brother, but decided not to. I couldn't risk him blurting it out to Pa that I had spoken to Michael.

"Hello ... Hello?" I felt a shiver run down my shoulders and upper back, and my skin broke out in goosebumps.

"Hey! Michael ..." Kevin began, and my heart began to pound like a jackhammer. I made a move for the phone but Kevin waved me away. He was frowning.

"Huh? Already? Okay, okay."

Down went the goosebumps, sinking back into my skin.

"Can you ask if Michael knows ..." Kevin was seemingly interrupted by whoever was speaking on the other end.

"Hey, do you know where ... Oh, you don't? Hey, can I add you to my ... Hello? Hello?"

Kevin put the phone down and looked at me apologetically.

"Sorry. We're too late."

I had to think of something. Quickly. What else could I do to reach Michael before Mum left?

"Do you know anyone who might know him or where he is?"

"No, I don't."

"Are you sure?"

"I don't know his friends. You should know more about that than me."

"Why should I know that?"

"Well, you're his brother! Maybe his friends have been to your house before?"

"Well, yeah, a few of them. I would recognise them if I saw them somewhere but I don't remember their names ..."

"Do any of these guys look familiar?" Kevin held out the phone to me again. The screen showed four guys posing in front of an array of drums and guitars. They were a scruffy bunch, all of them with long straggly hair and faces marked with bright-red acne. Dressed in torn jeans and black shirts emblazoned with the names of bands I'd never heard of before, like "Ass Bites Snake" and "The Suck", they stood with their arms folded in a tight, sombre stance. The most striking of the lot was the one on the far left, who stood a head taller than the rest, his pale complexion making his pimples look all the more obvious.

"Mmmph, ha ha … He looks so weird," I found myself sniggering. "He grew his hair! He's in a band!"

"Yeah, they call themselves *Astragah*. They're shit."

"No surprises there."

I studied the faces of Michael's band mates closely. "No, I don't know the other three."

The picture had a comments section below it, and there were three entries posted there, all of them barely understandable, none of them useful. One of the posts looked like it had been written by a band mate of Michael's, one Ahmad Ponteng. I recognised him from the photo I had just seen of the band. Clicking on his name took us to a page that showed his profile picture in full: an afro-haired goon whose ears looked less like they had got a professional piercing job and more like he'd gone to a stationery shop and got them ring-bound, two for the price of one. Then there was another picture that showed a side view of him, topless, his arm flexed and holding a guitar as if it were a dumbbell. It might have looked mildly impressive if it hadn't been for the fact that his elbow was being supported by a rather substantial belly, and that there was an equally substantial tuft of hair on said belly, curling around his navel then extending downwards into his sweatpants.

Because Kevin wasn't "friends" with this fellow, our access to his page was restricted and these images were the only reward we got for our inquisitive efforts. This was hopeless. I sighed and slumped down on my bunk. Kevin clicked on a few more photos on Michael's profile, but they only showed my brother doing stupid things like hugging a motorcycle or standing in front of a fast food restaurant. Besides, these photos didn't have any comments to provide us with any additional leads. The only thing I had learned from them was that even after many weeks of not seeing Michael, I was still sick of the sight of his face.

Now what? Phoning or messaging him was all but out of the question, and I didn't hold out much hope for sending him an e-mail. The only thing left to do was to go meet him in person. But where was he? Nobody knew. And there was a bigger problem: even if I knew where Michael was, how exactly would I get there? In a country with practically non-existent public transport and taxi services, the only way I could ever get to Michael's place was to be driven out there by my father. And there was as much chance of that happening as there was of Michael's band winning a Grammy.

Kevin, sensing that he'd done enough for it to count as amends, climbed back onto his bunk, and he took his phone with him. I stretched my back and scratched a leg, feeling just as restless as I had before I saw the confirmation of Michael talking to my mother.

"Hey, Jonathan, look!" Kevin's head appeared over the edge of his bunk again, and he handed me his phone. I steadied myself as I took it, trying not to get too hopeful.

I found myself looking at the very first photo I had seen, the one with the band lined up in front of their instruments. Except now, there were two more comments underneath it, posted only a minute ago. The first was from Ahmad Ponteng, asking, in what was barely discernible as English, about when and where a certain get-together was to be held tomorrow. This was answered by a "Michael Lee", confirming that the meeting was to happen at Friendly Garden Pool Centre at 1.30 p.m. A search on the name of the place directed me to an address: Unit 32, *Simpang* 64, Jln. Badir.

Badir was a relatively recent development and I'd only ever been there a few times, usually to eat out with Pa and the others on the days we got sick of instant noodles and food from the *ringkat* delivery service we relied on for most of our dinners. Badir was an unimportant commercial district only a short drive from the capital, so it wasn't too far away from here, but getting out of the house was still going to be impossible. Michael may as well have been in space for all it mattered. It was all the same. I was never getting out, never in a million years, let alone in less than a day's time.

Unaware of the damage he'd further done, Kevin cheerfully plucked the phone off my hands and returned to a good night's sleep. I sighed and lay down, putting my pillow over my face to cover my eyes, but then pulling it away immediately. Crap, it was still wet with my tears.

Chapter Six

I was sitting in my classroom. The same old place I went to five days a week, every week, where two out of the four ceiling fans didn't work, and there were desks covered in graffiti, either carved in with compasses or drawn in Tipp-Ex, cockroaches lurking about in the cubbyholes, mice in the dustbin, and thirty-four children sitting crammed together to have a textbook dictated to them word for word for two hours straight.

Only, everything had suddenly become wonderful, and the classroom was now as good as heaven on earth. No more Mrs. Yap and her tyranny or Mr. Shah and his tedious lectures on civic-mindedness; our new teacher was my mother, back from her break in sunny Melbourne. And everyone in my class loved her, as they obviously would.

The only problem was that I couldn't see her face. Her back was turned to me the entire time she solved the problems on the blackboard, and when she read us stories, her whole head remained hidden behind the book. It was strange that no matter how much I shifted my body or inched myself closer, her face continued to evade me. Like trying to pull a surprise on the boy in the mirror, anything I attempted was futile. I knew I had to be patient. But at least the story was a good one, and one that I knew Mum liked to tell. We had got to the part where Procrustes invites his guest up to his special room when my mother finally began to lower her book to look at me.

And then the alarm rang in my ears. It was 6.30 a.m. I was back in Kevin's room.

Though most of the details slipped away into the widening gulf between my dreaming and waking, I managed to keep hold of a picture of everyone sitting in my classroom, all smiles, writing away with black pens and instantaneously grasping those unfathomable concepts of functions and integers that usually stumped us. Now, no fraction was too hard, no multiplication too complicated. My Mum explained things so well that we were all like sponges dropped into a swimming pool, soaking up every bit of mathematical knowledge that flowed our way. Then on to English, and her telling of the tale, of Procrustes the innkeeper and his wonderful bed that could always fit every traveller, no matter how tall or short they came to his door. What a shame the alarm clock went off before she could finish and then give me a glimpse of what I had missed for six months.

After three successive beeps, Aaron shut the alarm off and began to stir, while I tried to re-enter the dream, despite knowing full well that it would never work. If I did get back to sleep at all, it would be with a completely new reverie, and most likely one that wouldn't have Mum in it.

I brought my mother's face up in my mind. No, I hadn't quite forgotten it yet. How could I? She hadn't been gone that long, after all. Six months was a mere ... 5% of the life I had lived so far? Didn't seem that big in the grand scheme of things. But with my waking came something else, something I hadn't felt before, not even on the night my mother had left, and it felt even worse than the *geram* from last night. It was a pang, a longing in my chest that went so deep and came on so acutely the instant I was fully awake that it left me unable to get myself off the bed, or even move my body in the hope of somehow shaking it off. If the *geram* had been a stirring up of my insides, then this was like an implosion, a black hole sucking out all my defences and leaving behind a vast emptiness that all the yearning in the world would never have filled.

I brought a hand to my chest and rubbed on it to ease the ache, but that only brought back a memory of when I'd fallen ill with a bad flu last year. The fever had led me into a terrifying dream in which I'd found myself on a collapsing staircase that was crumbling down and falling forever through an infinite sky. It was Mum who had jolted me awake and out of that agonisingly endless plummet by bringing a hand to my brow to wipe off my perspiration. She had then adjusted my blanket so I was warm but not stifling, stroked my flushed cheek to comfort me, and then made me sip from a fresh jug of water until I was settled once more. The dream never returned, and I had slept undisturbed for the rest of that night.

In many ways, what I was experiencing now was at least as bad as that hellish nightmare I'd suffered a year ago, but this time Mum wasn't there beside me to make things better. There was no soothing hand against my forehead to let me know that there was something to hold on to in the darkness. No warm body against mine, offering nothing but kindness and reassurance and the chance to hug back as tightly as I could and never let go. No soft, graceful voice to tell me that no matter how scared or helpless I felt, it would all be alright in the morning.

One way or another, I had to find out. I had to find out today, or else it would be like this day after day after day, and I couldn't bear to face this feeling for even one second more. If I didn't do something, I might lose her forever, just like Kevin had said I would.

The pain dulled only a bit as I finally managed to pull myself out of bed and changed into my official mourning clothes, and then headed over to breakfast, which was a routine wordless affair. The adults were also fully clad in their own mourning outfits, to be worn for the rest of the funeral: the men wore white shirts and black trousers while *Ah Em* was completely covered in black. Over their clothes they had on vests fashioned out of some type of coarse beige-coloured material, which looked like the stuff used to make gunny sacks.

The silence at the breakfast table was, however, soon broken by the arrival of our aunt and her husband. It started with the sound of their honking car from outside the house, and was followed by a flurry of activity from the funeral room, the chattering and flapping about between them and *Ah Peh* bursting into the kitchen through its thin walls.

I anticipated a brilliant climax to the commotion outside, and I wasn't disappointed. A ninja crashed through the doorway suddenly, startling all of us.

"I came as soon as I could!" our aunt gasped, panting heavily. She was clothed in black from the neck down, and her outfit even had a black hood-like accessory that she'd pulled over her head.

"Hello, *Ah Koh,*" we chorused. Pa muttered a greeting to his sister and invited her to have some cold tuna sandwiches with us.

"Ugh, no thanks. My lymphatic system is still negatively charged and I haven't oxidised my colon yet, yah," she responded rather calmly before breaking into a wail. "How did it happen? He was only in for his chest! How, Seng? Were you there?"

Pa gave a very subtle, disapproving twist of one corner of his mouth. "No, Ming, I wasn't there. You'll have to ask Soon."

"I was giving a presentation on how to charge your brain magnetically for my 'Holistic Mind Achievers' course when I got the message. It was so terrible! I burst into tears right there in the middle of the room! And I felt him, Seng, I did! At that moment! Going up and up … And then I looked up and raised my arm out to our father …" *Ah Koh* sighed deeply and lifted up her arms for dramatic effect.

Our aunt's husband, Uncle Ben, popped up behind her.

"Hi, Chin Seng. Hi, kids," he greeted. He always insisted that we call him "Ben" rather than "*Koh Teoh*". Our compromise was to address him as "Uncle Ben". The weird part was that his name wasn't even Ben; it was Beng Huat. "Ben" was apparently something he'd come up with after getting together with my aunt. Whatever floated his boat; who was I to argue with someone who was a lecturer at the university and had a PhD in Physics.

Uncle Ben and *Ah Koh* had met while studying in New Zealand, and they were a couple of years into their married life, or the "ball and chain" as he liked to put it to me. I often wondered who the ball was and who the chain.

"Hey, guys." Uncle Ben pulled up a chair and squeezed himself between Kevin and me, nudging his big moon-cheeked face into ours as close as he could. "It's tough, isn't it? But don't you worry. Ben is here to make things all better. Any time you kids need me, I'll be there."

"Yeah, thanks," I said as I edged away from him.

"You guys don't have to be sad, okay. Your grandpa's gone off to a special place. He's up there now, smiling down on all of us …" Uncle Ben broke off to stifle a sob. "Excuse me … He's … up there with God and …" Uncle Ben couldn't hold it back, and trailed off into a high-pitched squeal that ended in uncontrollable sobbing. *Ah Koh* went to his side and embraced him, rubbing his back in the same way a mother would do to burp her baby.

"Aww, poor Benny ... Yes, he's gone to a better place. No more suffering."

"Unghh ... Oh no, it's happening again ..." Ben mumbled, weeping readily into *Ah Koh*'s sleeve.

"Uncle Ben, you know, we kids are here for you if you need anything," offered Kevin. This made our uncle cry even harder, and *Ah Koh* had to lead him away to help him recover.

In addition to being considerably younger than her two brothers, *Ah Koh* looked and acted nothing like them. Quick-tempered and impulsive, she was used to speaking her mind whenever she felt like it and always got the last word in with anyone in the family, aided in no small part by her status as the baby of her generation. As the eldest, *Ah Peh* probably still got the final say in most things that involved him and his siblings, but I'd heard him complain more than once that he'd gone half-deaf in one ear after years of listening to his sister's incessant nattering.

She did make a good physical match for Uncle Ben though, both of them quite short and with the same petite builds and similarly rounded faces. They even had matching squints, though her eyes went in divergent directions while Uncle Ben's pointed inwards.

After *Ah Koh* and Uncle Ben left to settle in, *Ah Peh* and *Ah Em* reiterated last night's briefing about the day ahead. We were expecting relatives from the extended family, as well as family acquaintances and associates from the Chinese Chamber of Commerce, so everyone was going to have to pitch in and attend to the guests. We kids were specifically instructed to be as discrete as possible as we went about doing our chores. Also, we had to make sure to look as sad as possible at all times, especially in the presence of visitors. Aaron and I were allotted the most menial of jobs, ones where we'd be the least conspicuous, like arranging the shoes that had been taken off by the guests into neat lines and helping prepare the refreshments.

Some guests did arrive early, soon after we had finished breakfast. Among the first to walk in through the front door were a couple of *Ah Kong*'s friends, my uncle's and Pa's colleagues, a few fourth-degree relatives, and some of the neighbours. They all streamed into the living room to say a prayer at the altar and their farewells to *Ah Kong*'s body, and then stayed on a bit for a drink and to offer a few words of condolences to the adults of the family. Those within the family's inner circle were expected to arrive the next day for the actual ceremony that would precede the burial, although a few of them were expected to be dropping by today as well.

I went about my duties perfunctorily, and garnered little attention or comment from the guests. From what I'd seen in the mirror last night, looking like the world was about to end came quite naturally to me, which made keeping up the sad front, as requested by the adults, a piece of cake.

My brother carried on too, looking much like I did, still plenty subdued from the previous night's commotion. I hadn't said anything to him since the incident. I got the feeling that he wanted to be left alone, and this kept me from approaching him. Kevin seemed toned down as well, but that was probably because he was being forced to accompany his father from group to group and engage in the customary small-talk that *Ah Peh* had to make as host.

The intense yearning I'd felt for my mother when I had woken up had diminished a little, but it still remained as a constant throbbing ache – this was of course preferable to what had started as a great big hole torn into my chest. But I was all too aware of it, the yawning chasm inside me, and the more I thought about it, the more fixated I became on an image of Mum stepping into a plane and leaving for good, never to return. The image flashed before my eyes again and again, and as the morning wore on, I grew less and less able to focus on the tasks I was supposed to do. Twice I had to be not-so-gently prodded into getting back to work by my father, after he spotted me standing around and staring vacantly into space.

When the streams of visitors began thinning out a little, I took the opportunity to head out somewhere, away from all the funeral stuff, so I could get my head in order and clear out my thoughts. And I knew the perfect place for doing this.

I went into the dining area, and then into the house's wet kitchen, where *Ah Peh*'s servants were preparing lunch. It was spacious, and probably had the capacity to produce enough food for several armies (or one Kevin). To one side, I saw a large pot sitting on one of the gas hobs, filled with boiling pork broth, and next to it was a giant wok that one of maids was using to stir-fry long beans and carrots. To the opposite end of the kitchen were two other maids standing by a countertop, preoccupied with chopping up a steamed chicken and peeling flecks of meat off the carcass. I slipped by unnoticed, and then went through the door that opened out to the house's backyard.

Kevin's house had a sizable compound, but most of it was in front and to the sides. Here, at its rear, it was merely at a ten-metre distance from the backdoor to the chain fence that encircled the property. In one corner of the yard stood a group of jackfruit trees overlooking a vegetable patch where the servants cultivated chillies and string beans. In the other corner rested an old, faded plastic swing-and-slide set meant for preschoolers, set up back when Kevin and I were toddlers and long since disused. And then there was the cage, right in front of me, the centrepiece of the backyard and kept well out of the glare of the sunlight by two leafy mango trees.

It was a generously sized cage, about three by three metres or so, and was essentially an extension of the main fence but with a door built into it. Pak Tut squatted in the middle of it, basking in the warm morning sun, his slender head darting about, his eyes fixed on the many dot-sized bugs buzzing around him. Roughly a metre and a half long, nose to tail, he was as handsome a specimen of monitor lizard as any I'd ever seen, with smudges of brown and black strewn all over his murky, dark green coat. I liked reptiles, and I especially liked Pak Tut; he was one of the few things I truly looked forward to whenever I visited my uncle's house.

Watching Pak Tut go about his business would help me get my mind off Mum and all that had happened yesterday, at least for a while. There was something I liked about the way he carried himself; even if it was just a small enclosure, he strutted around like the king of his own little world, and without a care for whatever was outside the borders of his realm.

Sadly, my respite didn't last long. Not more than a minute after I had got here, Kevin appeared at the door, holding out his phone.

"Jonathan! There you are!" he panted, red-faced and sweaty.

"What happened to you? Run a cross-country?"

"No, I ran here from upstairs. Call for you."

He handed it to me gingerly, and I passed him a look of suspicion in return.

"Call for me on your phone?"

"Don't take too long."

"Okay."

As I'd suspected, it was Radzi, my best friend, who'd rung to ask when I'd be coming back to school.

"The burial's tomorrow, so probably the day after that."

"You're so damn lucky. We're getting two spot tests tomorrow, man."

"You don't have to worry. You always score above 90% anyway."

"Hey, come on, Jonathan."

Despite giving me the impression that he was in a great hurry, Kevin remained at the doorway, listening in on my conversation with great interest. Pak Tut swivelled his body around and began making lethargic strides to his little wooden hut at the far side of the cage.

"Why are you calling Kevin's phone, anyway? How did you know I was with him?"

"Everyone knows your grandfather died, *bah*. I figured you'd be at Kevin's house since that's where you told me your *Ah Kong* stayed when he was alive," he explained earnestly. "Besides, the landline's engaged."

I decided to let it go. It wasn't inconceivable that Radzi would have Kevin's mobile number. I probed him, instead, about any interesting classroom gossip or shenanigans that my friends might have been up to while I was away. It was heartening to learn that I'd not missed anything.

"So, did you get a chance to ask Hong Wee about those

firecrackers?"

"Huh? No, but he did say that his cousin's coming back from Miri in a few days so I guess we'll know then."

"We should tell his cousin that we want proper air bombs this time. Like the ones that go ..."

Kevin walked up to me and stopped just short of stepping on my toes. He glared at me, and then pointed to his phone.

"Radzi, I've got to go now. Kevin's asking for his phone back."

"Oh ... Alright, dude. One more thing: we'll probably be sitting the topical tests next week so you should start revising," my friend said from the other end.

"Great ... Yeah, okay." Kevin was still standing close, his face almost touching mine. "See you. Better get back before recess finishes."

"Yeah. Bye, Jonathan."

I hung up and handed the phone back to my cousin.

"I should charge you for that call," he said scornfully, cradling the device as if shielding it from a (my) malicious presence.

"Get a life, Kevin. And do you have to stand so close? I can smell your breath."

"Hah, very funny. You know, we're lucky the guests have stopped coming in for now. I had to spend the whole morning with them."

"Looked like a lot of fun."

"Yeah, right ..." Kevin said drily. "By the way, the thing ... It's arrived."

"What thing?" Then, I figured out what he was talking about. "Oh! It has? Did you see it?" I asked. He nodded gleefully.

"It was long and black but curved like a boat. It's not straight like the ones we see on TV."

I tried to picture the casket as my cousin described it. Like a boat, huh? Was that not what the Vikings used to bury their dead? A vessel on which the deceased would embark on a new journey into the afterlife.

"Want to have a look? It's at the front of the house."

"Sure, yeah ..."

Obviously, I'd never seen a coffin in real life, but, like Pak Tut, it would be another distraction to keep me from thinking about Mum, at least for a little while longer.

I tailed my cousin, clearing a corner of the house and trekking over the lawn in the process. There were flower beds and pots in every direction, bearing purple bougainvilleas and pale pink desert roses, not to mention the odd crimson hibiscus and bright yellow allamanda. In the background was a spread of fruit-bearing trees (mango, papaya, banana and even coconut) and all the assorted fauna that came with such a surplus of cultivation. Bees and butterflies flitted from flower to flower as little pipit birds chirped overhead, and I knew that if I had trained my eyes downwards and looked closely, I would have seen ants and beetles amidst the blades of grass, scrambling to get out of the way of our footsteps.

We reached a second corner and I peered around the concrete edge. The garden was separated from the driveway by a hedge of ixora bushes, and a white minivan was parked beside it, completely empty and all its doors open. Beside the minivan was a blue pickup truck, facing away from the house, which meant that it had probably been reversed into the driveway. It was pretty close, only a few metres from where we stood, affording me a good view of its interior and its long, broad bed that was covered by a plastic tarpaulin sheet. The driver was in the front seat, fast asleep, and another man, dressed in a pink, collared shirt, stood outside, speaking to *Ah Peh*.

"Oh, I think they've taken it in already," said Kevin, frowning. "The cover looks lower now."

Ah Peh and the other man went inside the house shortly, leaving us free to get closer to the truck without attracting any unwanted attention.

We approached the truck cautiously, and as I neared it, I began to feel my heart thumping in my ears like a red alert siren. What was I so anxious about? Getting discovered? Kevin's mother was an especially superstitious woman, and certainly wouldn't have approved of finding her son standing close to something as inauspicious as a coffin. I didn't think Pa would really care though, about me and Kevin gawking at coffins, but he would be angry that I was goofing around here when I could have been helping the others inside.

The part of the truck that wasn't visible from when we had first spotted it was now in view, and we saw that the truck bed was completely draped by the tarpaulin on this side as well. If we were going to see the coffins that were beneath the cover, assuming there were any, one of us would have to have to climb aboard and lift it out of the way.

"What do you think? Should we climb in?" I asked Kevin. He didn't respond, so I went ahead and moved closer, practically right up against the truck. And it was then that I noticed some writing printed along the base of the bed.

I hunched over to get a better look: most of it was written in Chinese, but one of the lines was in English. This was much smaller than the parts in Chinese, so I had to lean in to see until my nose was almost touching the truck.

I could not believe what I was seeing. A smile began spreading across my face and my heart welled up with hope, as if it were riding on a crest of optimism that I had no control over.

"Badir Enterprises Sdn. Bhd.," I read aloud.

And the company's address was printed alongside it too: *Simpang* 69, Jln. Badir. Only five *simpangs* away from the pool centre where Michael was going to be that afternoon.

"This is it. This will take me to Michael," I told Kevin.

"What? Are you crazy? That's the stupidest idea I've heard." Kevin was shaking his head vehemently. Was he right?

Sure, the address was close by, but would I be able to do it? And could I get away with it? It was now around 10.00 a.m., and Michael's meeting was at 1.30 p.m.; would it be possible for me to be out of the house for that long, and maybe longer, without having any of the adults find out? I felt the hope ebb away.

No, it was a stupid idea. Kevin was right. I was just a dumb kid with no money, no backbone and no chance of convincing my brother to do something I wanted even if I did manage to do the impossible and find him. Besides, why would Michael even help me out? He'd never been bothered about my happiness nor helped me with anything when he had been around, so why should he start now? And all of this was still assuming Mum hadn't flown away yet; for all I knew she was probably on the plane already.

"Hey, I think they're coming out!" Kevin warned. "Come on, let's go!"

I could hear *Ah Peh* and the man in the pink shirt speaking from inside the house; they were clearly nearing the front door, their voices growing louder.

I knew Pa would throw a fit if I left now. There were guests to attend to, and the funeral stuff to help out with if the others got tired. Lunchtime would be followed by another slew of people, who would hang around idly for hours, eating up all the refreshments we served them and asking us stupid questions like whether or not *Ah Kong* had been our favourite grandparent. It was only going to get busier from here on, and my help would be needed, so not only would my leaving be a dangerous and pointless feat but I'd be inconveniencing my family by getting on that truck as well.

I could now hear the gristly, creaking noise of the front door being opened; they'd be outside in seconds, and with a full view of us. No, it was certain that I'd be caught before the truck even left the premises. I'd just have to accept that I was never going to find out the truth about Mum; it'd remain a mystery forever, unsolved, like the Bermuda triangle, or why girls were so weird.

I would never know, would I? The yearning in my chest returned, this time like a fist clenched around my heart, trying to crush it to a pulp. Never, ever, ever ...

"Get out now, Jonathan! What are you doing?"

I had no idea what was happening, but I saw that my foot was already on the bottom rung of the mini-ladder set into the side of the truck, and I was hoisting myself up onto the bed, feet planting down firmly onto the edges of the tarpaulin. I could see the front entrance of the house, and the men standing behind the half-open door, *Ah Peh* with his hand on it and ready to open it fully at any moment.

"Get down! Don't act crazy!"

"I have to go!" My whole face felt like it was throbbing in tune to my racing heart, and so much sweat was collecting in my palms that I probably had enough to make a cup of Milo.

"I'll be back soon," I reassured Kevin although I didn't feel so sure myself.

"What makes you think you'll be able to find him? What if he doesn't show up?"

"It doesn't matter. I'm going to find him whether he's at the pool place or not. 'As long as I can get out of here, I can go anywhere'. That was what he said when he left home. Well, so can I. If he can do it, I can too."

"What?"

Ah Peh was opening the door all the way now; he pushed it a little each time he spoke, and this was accompanied by sporadic scrapes and squeaks, each of which prompted a twitch of panic in me. I couldn't afford to delay this anymore.

"Go back inside, Kevin! They're coming out!"

"But ..."

The door opened fully, and the man in the pink shirt stepped out first.

"Get out of here!"

Only to turn back, kneel and fasten his shoelaces.

"Kevin, I swear ..."

My cousin clasped his hands together as he bounced his upper body around on his little legs like he was trying to hold back a great flood of urine. From the corner of my eye I saw that my uncle had also stepped outside the house.

"Go! Now!"

Kevin stuck a hand into his pocket and plucked out his phone. After a brief fiddle here and there, he handed it to me.

"You might need this. I took down the keypad lock, so call if you need help," Kevin whispered, wiping his sweat off his brow.

"Uh, okay, thanks."

My cousin's act of kindness shocked me more than the

fortuitous discovery of the address on the truck had, and I was left speechless. By the time I had composed myself and was able to speak to him again, the sound of footsteps on the tiled patio got me darting straight under the tarpaulin, while Kevin dashed back to the rear of the house.

The cover was thankfully made of thinly-woven synthetic fibres, and it allowed for some sunlight to seep through, so there was no problem seeing what was around me. Three coffins lay together side by side, all smaller than what I'd expected, with their lengths allowing enough room for me to curl up not too uncomfortably at the tail end of the truck's bed. One of the coffins was black and covered in gold Chinese lettering and beautifully painted floral patterns, and had a curved, canoe-like shape that matched Kevin's description of *Ah Kong*'s coffin. The other two were plain, typically box-shaped and brownish and not unlike the coffins I had seen in movies.

They were all closed, and I started to wonder as to whether or not they might be occupied. My imagination couldn't help but run wild with the possibilities of what might be resting beneath the lids should I try to prise them open. Before I got the chance to act though, I heard them speak again, *Ah Peh* and the man in the pink shirt, and they sounded like they were standing very close to the truck.

"Make sure he remembers …" *Ah Peh* grumbled.

"Don't worry, Mr. Lee. I will," the other man replied. "Again, so sorry, but please understand. This has never happened to us before. We just got called to deliver two more, and we will have to drive all the way to …"

My uncle cut him off with something I couldn't fully hear, and then let his footsteps do the rest of the talking as he walked away from the truck. I heard the door of the truck's cab creak open and then slam shut.

"Wake up! Ricky, wake up! Come on, we have to hurry!" the man in the pink shirt yelled, and a few seconds later, the truck's engine came to life with a great explosion of diesoline fumes, which all too easily spilled into the back of the truck. I covered my mouth and nose and focused my energies into suppressing my every urge to cough and sneeze. I was already starting to worry: what if it was going to be like this the whole way? What if I couldn't breathe the whole time?

"As long as I can get out of here, I can go anywhere": those were Michael's infamous last words before he had slammed the door on us. And then opened it again to ask if Pa could drop him off in town, and perhaps help him pick up some instant noodles and gummy dinosaurs on the way.

Chapter Seven

The rattling was everywhere. I could feel it in my bones, my teeth, my hair, my ears. Any bumpier, I'd have spontaneously shattered like an opera singer's glass.

And it wasn't just me. The vibrations were being passed on to the coffins as well, which kept moving as long as the truck was in motion. Fortunately, they were too heavy to be flung about (like I might have been if I had not managed to hold on firmly to one of the side panels), but they did change position with each little jangle or shake of the truck, and it was disconcerting to see the trio of caskets edging themselves closer, sandwiching me between them and the rear wall of the bed. They hadn't been tethered or roped into place, and had their wood chipping off in bits and parts, which made me wonder about the quality of the specimen that had been submitted to our house a little while ago.

It didn't help that the back of the truck was extremely noisy and chokingly fume-filled; the first cloud of smoke the truck had let out had clearly not been the last of the vehicle's expulsions, and its foul releases continued to creep in from underneath the tarpaulin. My eyes constantly watered, and I had to snort away all the mucus building up in my nose every few minutes. I figured the men in front wouldn't be able to hear me through all noise the truck itself was making, so I didn't care to hold back. To make things even worse though, my motion sickness had kicked in again. It was a little better than how I felt while reading in a moving car, but that spinning sensation was beginning to grow ominously in my gut and in my head. I knew that once it had started, it would be a while before the feeling stopped or even eased off a bit. All I could do now was close my eyes tightly shut and hope that this was as bad as it was going to get.

Now, a typical drive from my uncle's house to Badir, in the absence of heavy traffic, would probably have taken a good twenty minutes. I opened my eyes to glance at Kevin's phone and took note: it was half an hour since the truck had left the house, and there was no indication of stopping as yet. The truck hadn't been making any major turns either, and there were plenty of cars passing us by, so we were probably still on the main road. Where exactly we were headed, I hadn't the faintest, but it increasingly looked like it wasn't Badir. There were other coffins inside the truck, so it seemed likely that these men would have a few more deliveries to make before returning to their home base.

The truck suddenly jerked to the right with a shrill screech of its tyres before coming to a complete stop, and the loud bursts of horns from the vehicles behind us blasted into my ears. I lost my grip and was thrown backwards; the sound was undeniably loud enough to reach the front, but hopefully the men were assuming it to be from one of the coffins tossing about. As I rubbed my sore elbow, I heard an engine rev up on the truck's left. "*Hoi! Kalantit! Kau punya palir*!" barked the pink-shirted man from the front of the truck. Whatever vehicle had being trying to cut into our path zoomed off, but not before letting out a new cloud of smog in our direction. I almost gave myself away by breaking into a coughing fit, then buried my face into my sleeve just in time and choked it down as best I could.

The truck began moving again, slowly picking up pace, and I stretched out all my limbs like a spider, using each one to grab or press on to any available surface I could find, including the coffins. One of them, a rectangular light-brown model, had slid in towards me; it was still aligned more or less along the length of the truck bed, but had been pushed in so close that I could barely extend both of my elbows outwards at the same time, wedged in as I was and getting forced slowly into a tighter, narrower squeeze.

Before I could get comfortable with my new position, the truck started making a few winding turns, moving on to considerably rockier ground in the process. I realised that we had finally veered off the main road and felt relieved that we were probably getting closer to our destination. My relief rapidly turned to agony, however, when the vibrating that I'd just about got used to tripled-over in intensity as the truck rattled on along the rougher roads, and soon even the sound of my breathing came off like the buzzing of a horde of angry bees. The coffins, likewise, shook even more and made larger jumps, inching closer and closer and wedging me against the wall. I gritted my teeth and clenched my eyelids shut more tightly, but I knew that was hardly going to help. The first solid waves of proper nausea began rolling across my stomach and towards my throat, and I began to make small, intermittent burps.

The truck finally began to slow down, and the sounds of traffic I had been hearing around me all along faded out to almost complete silence. The tyres sloshed against the ground beneath us, and then the truck rolled to a stop. I heard the two men at the front of the truck open their doors, followed by the guy in the pink shirt barking out an order: "Hey, Ricky! Take off the cover and help them take out 235B!"

The words chilled me to my bones, as did the sound of the men stepping out and onto the ground. I had to think fast. There was no escape out of the truck, and there was no rational explanation I could give them about why I was hitching a ride with their precious cargo. One of them, presumably Ricky the driver, was fast approaching me; any closer and he would be able to hear me moving underneath the tarpaulin. There was only one thing I could do, and I jumped straight into it without a second thought.

There were three coffins available for me to choose from, and only one would be unloaded by the men. Which one was 235B? There was no time to look for numbers or codes. I had to act quickly. The light brown one that had been displaced the most during the drive, nearly squashing me flat as a result, was the nearest one within my reach, and also looked the least heavy of all. I prised open the lid (which was a lot weightier than anticipated but just about manageable) and shot straight inside the coffin, pressing myself against the white, cushioned interior and closing shut the casket after me, hoping with all my might that my hiding place wasn't 235B.

The driver climbed onto the truck bed almost as soon as I'd made my move. I heard the muffled sounds of him grabbing on to the handles of the coffin I was lying in, and then I felt the sensation of being dragged across the truck bed. Shit! This was it. He was going to take this coffin out of the truck, and I would be caught out in front of a grieving family, and they'd all find me lying there, looking stupid and scared. I started desperately coming up with a number of excuses to give them as to how I got inside the coffin, while also considering the option of making a break for it the instant the lid came off. I'd have the element of surprise,

I reasoned, and this might help make up for my uselessness as a speed-runner.

Fortunately, the need for that never came to pass. The shifting halted before I was moved out of the truck completely, and instead, I felt another person clamber up onto the bed to drag out one of the other coffins. I relaxed.

It was pretty warm inside the coffin, and the cushions weren't exactly the most comfortable to lie on, but there was plenty of room for me and it was almost 100% soundproof – it felt much better in here than the noisy rattling of the truck bed outside.

Perhaps, I should just stay in here, I considered. I brought out Kevin's phone to light up the interior of my coffin: nothing but white cushion everywhere, including overhead, lining the lid. This might just be the last thing I would ever see, I thought suddenly, on the off chance that I couldn't get out and was buried alive in here. My mouth went dry, and I didn't feel very comfortable anymore. I had to get out of the coffin as soon as I could. Some minutes later, the hum of the truck's engine revved back to life, and we headed off again, although I still didn't know where exactly we were going. I waited until I was confident that the vehicle was well on its way, and then I gently pushed the lid off, stepping back out onto the truck bed.

The tarpaulin has been re-draped but not secured properly, and it was left wide open at the back where I was, a couple of feet from the truck's rear. As I scrambled out, I noticed that a white sports car was tailing us quite closely, and it seemed for a moment that its driver would see me and my game would be up. But then I saw that the man driving the car was too busy texting on his phone to be paying attention to the road or to the boy standing on the truck bed right in front of him. I rushed to grab on to the free end of the sheet while I had the chance, pulling it down just as his eyes flicked forwards, and managing to catch a brief glimpse of him tossing his phone into the back of the car in shock and jumping up in his seat violently enough to knock his head on the car roof before I was fully covered once more, and out of sight from the outside world.

Hopefully, this was my last near-miss, I thought to myself, curling back down against the side of the truck's bed, and feeling the adrenaline rush from all the recent excitement ebb away, only to be replaced again by the rather familiar feeling of motion sickness that was threatening to make me puke my guts out. It was just my luck that the only cure for it seemed the prospect of a near-death experience or some such. Regardless, I started trying to think about how I would make my way to Badir. The phone provided a sobering wake-up present: it was 11.15, over an hour into my journey. We could've been almost anywhere in Brunei right now, and almost certainly not anywhere near where I was meant to be. The bleakness of the situation was dawning on me the further we kept driving. Was the truck even going to Badir? What if it was taking me in the opposite direction? And even if it did end up in Badir, how long would it take for us to get there? How I wished I'd brought along something for luck, like my trusty G2 black pen. That would surely have offered some protection against the gods of misfortune.

The truck slowed down and turned to the left, again moving over an uneven earthen track. Like before, the increased bumpiness made my motion-sickness skyrocket in intensity. One way or another, it was time for me to make an exit, before I got any further away from Badir, and before the nausea could kill me by either making me vomit out my organs or making my head explode. Perhaps both at the same time; it was that bad.

But how was I going to walk out of the truck unnoticed?

We come to a stop, and the men climbed out. There was no detectable chatter this time around, but I did hear the sounds of someone approaching the truck bed, so I scurried back into the brown coffin. This time, the urgency of the moment did not help alleviate the problem rumbling in my stomach, and a salty-sour taste began to grow at the back of my throat. Vomiting was imminent, and it was going to be inside this small space.

No! I had to resist, or at least avoid doing it in there. I clamped both hands over my mouth and focused hard on mentally pushing down what was rising back. I was salivating profusely now, and beginning to feel that telltale gagging at the back of my throat. At the same time, I managed to catch the faint sounds of the tarpaulin being unravelled, but I was now past worrying about being discovered. Throwing up in three, two, one …

With an almighty retch, I gave in and let it all out onto the coffin's interior. Almost disappointingly, there didn't seem to be that much to expel; I'd only had half a sandwich for breakfast and a glass of water. Most of it was the saliva that had been pooling in my mouth, and I could feel a generous amount of residual drool dribbling down my lip. Instinctively, I brought a sleeve up to wipe it away, but then changed my mind and instead rubbed my mouth against the coffin's lining closest to my face. It was already soiled so a little more wouldn't make much of a difference.

Having a good hurl had greatly relieved my nausea, but after coming to my senses, I realised that the unpleasantness was not over. The men had not done anything about the coffins since removing the cover. I was in the dark, quite literally, as to what was going on outside and how much longer I could afford to remain inside the coffin. Add to that the growing stuffiness and the idea of being surrounded in my own sick, whose rancid smell I was starting to pick up and getting a bit queasy about … No, I couldn't stay a moment longer.

Slowly, I lifted the lid up. A thin ray of light streamed in, along with a faint but refreshing burst of air. There were no startled exclamations or frightened shrieks, so I felt safe enough to open it a bit more.

Further up went the lid, enough for me to peer through the gap. The tarpaulin had been taken off as I'd suspected, and I looked out: I saw a clearing with what looked like a small warehouse and fencing at the far end. The ground was also visible and had the appearance of yellow-brown mud, grainy like sand and gravel mixed together. Otherwise, the place was devoid of any visible signs of life, and all was still around me. There wasn't going to be a better moment to escape, so I decided to brave it and get myself off the truck.

I crawled out carefully, feet first, leaving my back and shoulders to prop up the coffin's lid as my lower half worked to gain a foothold on the truck bed. My heart was pounding and even the tiniest suggestion of noise or movement from beyond my very restricted field of view brought me to the brink of abandoning my attempt to flee and return to the confines of the casket.

Then, in an instant, I was out. The coffin lid snapped shut behind me as I dropped onto the truck bed, and I made a leap off it, landing with a loud "thump" on the hard-packed dirt of the crude parking lot, the impact nearly forcing my feet out of their sandals and causing me to almost topple over. Without looking back, I broke into a run, stumbling a little, my sandals throwing up gritty dirt everywhere and wedging the stuff in between my toes.

When I had reached a reasonably safe distance away from the truck, I allowed myself to slow down into a walk. I was on a track leading out of the area, and was looking back at the truck that was still parked in front of the small warehouse. It seemed like I had made a successful escape after all; the continuing lack of activity behind me was clear proof of it.

It was only a few metres more before I had cleared the gateway set into the surrounding wire fence. Several signs hung from the open gate, listing among other things the name of the company, the Badir office address that had led me to get on the truck in the first place, and the address of a warehouse – probably the one I was in, and it was definitely not anyplace close to Badir, or even the district I lived in. Served me right for making such a big assumption with the name and the address. Kevin's phone read 11.25, and here I was in the middle of nowhere and with no clue as to how to get to Badir. Maybe I could ask the guys who had driven the truck here? They wouldn't know that I was a stowaway, and I could just give them the address and maybe they'd take me there.

I turned back to the warehouse, almost decided on going back, but saw just in time that the men were re-entering the truck and starting the engine. The vehicle roared back to life and hurtled towards the gate at full speed, unconcerned with the potential damage to the coffins on board or the boy standing in front of them, about to be run over. I could have tried getting in front of the truck to get them to stop for me, but I instead went with my instincts and scampered to the side, out of the way of the truck, which then sped by, leaving behind a cloud of dust in my face.

Hacking out grainy spit, I stood there, trying to bat away the dirt out of my eyes and cursing those crazy idiots who had either not seen me or had not cared about squashing me into road-kill.

Well, if they'd killed me, they'd probably have simply scooped me off the road and packed me in one of their coffins, just one more customer to add to their books, and gone ahead on their merry way.

Chapter Eight

After walking around for a while to confirm there was no-one left there to ask for help, I went on my way, leaving behind the warehouse and going down the only path left for me to take.

My surroundings seemed like untouched jungle, filled with ominously primitive flora: tall, stick-like trees that bore no fruit and masses of ferns with all their multi-fingered fronds emerged from a marshy ground that was completely covered in long blades of grass almost as tall as I was. The artificial path I was on merged with the marsh on both sides, and water weeds aplenty peeked out from the sodden earth, around which dragonflies adorned in brilliant crimson and mosquitoes the size of fruit pastilles skittered and circled about.

I kept going, and soon arrived at a small sawmill and a scrap-metal heap. Given my circumstances, they did seem like viable options for me to get help, but after a moment's thought, I decided against doing that. This was partly (but in no small way) influenced by a movie I had watched with Kevin and his father on New Year's Eve, about a lumberjack killer whose main hobby was to kidnap unsuspecting children and use the tools in his private mill to chop them up in all kinds of creative ways.

I walked on. The day had gone a bit cloudy and cooler, making my trek just that little bit more bearable. To take my mind off my desolate surroundings, I put myself on the lookout for any interesting distractions I could find in the area. A few metres up from the sawmill, I encountered one: a small hut on stilts that would barely fit a grown man inside. It was a *durung*, a traditional store where farmers had once stored their crops and foodstuffs, mainly sago flour. Where the stilts had been inserted into the base of the hut, wooden circular discs had been attached, curved downwards on their sides. I'd read about these in a geography book: they were there to keep rats from getting in. The *durung*'s presence here was fascinating but not altogether inconceivable. If one paid careful attention, one could occasionally find such antiquated relics scattered randomly across the landscape, even along highways and otherwise heavily built-over residential areas. When development progressed as patchily as it did in Brunei, things tended to get bypassed by the tides of change. Including gems like this *durung*, gems that were sadly getting rarer with each passing month and year. It was probably inevitable that at some point they would all be swept away, out into the wastes of time, submerged forever within the memories of people who had passed on.

The *durung* indicated the existence of a past settlement in these parts, and I began to wonder if there were even more interesting things I could chance upon here, like, say, a longhouse or a collection of heads left behind by a head-hunter. How cool would that be! I could wear those mummified heads around my neck like a trophy or hang them on my door as the ultimate "keep-out" sign for my room.

I wasn't so fortunate though. All I found were a couple of abandoned stilt houses with zinc roofs and no air-conditioning units, not far off from the *durung*. They'd clearly been uninhabited for ages, their state of crumbling disuse a dead giveaway, along with their faded paint and rotting frames. One even looked like it might have caught (or been set on) fire at one point. I briefly toyed with the prospect of venturing into them to see if they contained any treasure I could take back home with me, but I was pressed for time and they were too far into the marsh for my sandals to manage the walk there.

There was another abandoned house a bit further down from the two stilt houses, much larger than them and closer to the track. It was a two-storied structure, with multiple broken glass windows and a badly rusted awning that ran full circle between its upper and lower levels. A small ring of bare earth surrounded it, and was connected to the track by a narrow, dry dirt-path. Whatever colour the house had once been painted in had long weathered away; all that remained now was the dark brown of the wooden planks that formed its main structure, and the coppery-red of the badly oxidised metal sheets that formed its roof.

This house I stopped for; I couldn't help but stay and stare at it. The clouds above me had by now gathered into a vast, hulking mass of dark grey, blocking out the sun and giving not just the house but the entire landscape an ominous feel. Its upper floor loomed overhead against the overcast sky, and its two glassless windows stared down at me like the empty sockets of a skull. Below, the house's door-less entrance resembled the gaping maw of a monster, its screaming laugh frozen in wood, daring any passerby to meet their doom inside.

A thunderclap rang out, and I looked up. A drop of water fell on me, straight into my eye. I flinched, wiped it off and by the time my hand was off my face, rain was falling everywhere. With no other shelter in sight, I forced my leaden legs to make a move and ran across the path, which had already turned into a thick greyish mud that clogged the soles of my sandals, and into the house.

As I walked in, I found myself in a short corridor, looking into an open hall, dimly lit thanks to the downpour outside but bright enough for me to tell that the plaster on the walls was mostly intact, although marred with peelings, bubbles and discolouration. The ceiling was similarly cracked in most places, and had an unsettling fat bulge towards its middle, where two rectangular fluorescent lights hung heavily and seemed to be dragging down the whole upper floor with them. The faint, musty smell of wood that had been wet for too long lingered in the air, and the floorboards were coated with reams of ancient dust. In terms of fixtures and furniture, there were none to be seen. What I did see instead was a hole in the middle of the hall's floor, big enough for me to squeeze into if I'd lost enough of my sanity to consider doing that.

Had the house been a totally stripped-down wreck with an interior that was completely destroyed and unrecognisable as a living space, I might have been more comfortable about venturing further in. But this still seemed a proper house; it was bare and rundown but definitely a house that had at one point or another been lived in by people. People who were no longer here. People who might now very well be dead.

I shuddered and proceeded towards the hall, slowly. I often scoffed at Kevin's fixation with ghosts and other things supernatural, but in all honestly I had an interest in spooky tales and the like as well, and did believe in the existence of such phenomena to a certain extent. Hence my wariness about a place like this, which was a dead ringer for any number of haunted houses I'd read about before.

I continued haltingly, watching out for any sudden movements by whatever horrid creatures that were occupying this ruin, ready to spring out of the woodwork at me at any moment. Ghosts were scary, of course, but perhaps all the more frightening were the filthy vermin that were most likely hiding out in every nook and cranny of the house, and the thought of getting overrun by swarms of them made bumping into a dead person's spirit seem quite preferable. The floor was awfully unsteady, and every few steps I made produced a series of rustling noises from both below and above me. Images of thousands upon thousands of little feet and claws scratching away behind the walls filled my mind, and I hoped that the sounds meant that whatever creatures were making them were clearing off and out of my way rather than preparing for an all-out assault.

Thankfully, the noises had subsided once I emerged into the hall proper. The lighting was still poor, but I could see a door directly ahead of me, closed shut, and there was a staircase next to it, rising to a pitch-black opening in the ceiling. I wasn't too keen on going up those stairs or to the upper floor, but curiosity did urge me to move nearer to see more of it.

And that's when I saw the cigarette butts. Little brown stubs that were littered around the bottom steps, as well as on the steps themselves. They weren't producing smoke anymore, but they didn't look that old either. I followed their trail down to the floor, and saw there were other things there besides the used cigarettes: chicken bones and apple cores, newspaper scraps, burnt out match sticks ... The place was a downright mess alright. A human-made mess. Which meant it had been made by someone who was living in the house. Someone who might still be in the house at this very moment ...

Suddenly, all didn't feel right. I looked towards the door of the room, and noticed that there was a line of cigarette butts leading up to it. I crept over to investigate, walking past the hole and practically treading on tiptoes. Once I got to the door, I stopped, leaned in, and put an ear as close as I could without touching it. I could not detect any signs of life inside, so I stood back up. After hesitating for a few moments, curiosity finally got the better of my fear, and I placed my hand on the knob and twisted it. It wasn't locked, and so the door creaked open. The room was seemingly empty, but even more dimly lit than the hall, so I would have to open the door wider to get a better look. And that I did, pushing the door open all the way.

I staggered back and almost fell to the floor at the scene before my eyes.

Hanging before me, from corner to corner and from edge to edge, were hundreds of wooden figurines, tied to a series of wooden rafters running across the ceiling. They were the size of a typical rag doll that any child would've chosen to play with, though few would have chosen one of these faceless, vaguely human-shaped effigies, many sporting gruesome mops of long, black, straggly, hair-like tendrils on their heads. And each one of the dolls, without any exception as far as I could see, had its body speared through by metallic rods the size of knitting needles, and had squares of red cloth marking the entry and exit points on their trunks.

What lay below them, on the ground, was just as shocking: sheets of newspapers covered the entire span of the room, all of them obituary pages, lined top to bottom over every inch of the floor. Faces upon faces stared up at me, the black-and-white portraits of all the deceased beckoning me to join their ranks, while overhead the impaled dolls swayed and rotated gently about their nooses, moved about by the rain and winds spilling into the room through its two smashed-up windows.

A gentle breeze drifted into the hall, its chilly touch glancing off the nape of my neck. I reached back instinctively to brush it off, and it felt like moving my hand through a column of icy air. I panicked. Whatever purpose all this had been done for, I had no desire to find out. Slowly, I began backing away, gently pulling the door shut, as if not to awaken the dolls, for they might have just been asleep and wouldn't be happy with being roused by a trespasser.

What followed next was not my first mistake of the day, but probably my first big one. Caught up in the act of backing off from the door, I forgot all about the one glaring obstacle that I would've been able to avoid had I thought to turn around. Instead, my stray foot planted itself into the hole in the middle of the hall's floor, throwing my body off balance. I jerked about trying to regain some stability, but then fell backwards, butt-first, crashing heavily down onto the floorboards with a deafening thud.

My pulse began to race palpably, and my eyes were darting about everywhere, scanning around wildly for any sign of an imminent attack. Lying in a heap on the floor, I braced myself, both physically and mentally for it. Something was surely going to happen now that I'd compromised my presence; nothing that loud could have escaped anyone or anything's notice. All I could do now was ready myself for my impending doom …

One second became two seconds became three and then sixty. A hundred. The stillness of the room remained undisturbed following my fall, and all there was to hear was the continued sound of the rain pouring down outside.

I pulled myself to a sitting position and my leg out of the hole. I rubbed at my foot; there was not even a scratch. All I had to worry about now was whether I'd accidentally landed on any of the disgusting trash littering the floor. Still sitting, I twisted to look over where I'd hit the ground; it was as dusty as the rest of the hall but mercifully nothing more than that.

There was just one small newspaper cutting lying beside me that, if anything, would've counted as a rare clean spot amidst a sweeping expanse of filth. It was another obituary, and it somehow hadn't made it into the other room. I'd already seen a hundred of those in there, so one more wasn't ...

Wait, I knew that face. It couldn't be ...

It was.

It was *Ah Kong*. His portrait, that same shot that was being used for the altar back at *Ah Peh*'s house, stared back at me, underscored by his date of birth and death, and the names of his living descendants. Including my name.

But that would mean ...

My train of thought went no further. The squealing groan of a door swivelling on its hinges rang out from above, a long, high-pitched wail that permeated the floorboards and walls and reverberated down the stairs.

I was out of there and back at the front door immediately.

But I couldn't step out of the house yet. The rain wasn't showing any signs of coming to a stop, and the path leading out of the house was almost submerged in murky water, along with much of the ground surrounding the house, which I would have to walk through.

The time was 11.40 a.m. Who knew when I might need to suddenly make a run for it? I decided to use this lull to take a bit of a breather to clear my head. After my experience inside, I didn't feel like sitting down once more, so I leaned against the frame of the doorway and rested my hand on the jamb, letting it take the full weight of my body while I took in a few deep breaths of fresh air. The moment I came into contact with it, however, I knew I'd made my second big mistake.

Even the faintest initial touch was enough for me to realise how badly rotten the wood was. But by then, it was too late. A good chunk of the jamb gave way, and then I fell down to the ground for the second time within barely five minutes.

For a brief moment, I thought that was going to be it. But then, a sinister scraping sound began to ring out from above me, while dust started to rain down almost as heavily as the real rain only inches away. The lintel overhead began to shudder and I readied myself for a fast break out of there. But it wasn't the lintel that gave way; it was the wooden underside of the house's awning. A good two metre chunk of it dropped to the rain-soaked earth with a splash, followed by pieces of grime and muck collected over years and years of neglect. Great clouds of it descended upon the doorway too, and then onto me as well.

"Oh crap!" I began dusting myself vigorously with the flats of my hands. Strange that the dirt seemed to be spreading on me rather than just getting brushed off. When I'd done enough of what I could, I leaned out to wash my hands clean in the rain, right below the broken awning. And as I stood there trying to get my hands and forearms wet only until my elbows, and no more, I heard a stirring noise from above. I couldn't help but look up.

And there it was, a whole hive of nesting bats, shivering from the sudden exposure, masses of leathery wings and matted fur moving in restless waves. Several looked down at me, their dog-like eyes and snouts fixed on the intruder standing below them. As I stood there, frozen in shock, a few more tilted their heads down, and then more and more joined in, rows and rows of glinting eyes appearing out of the dark swell of shifting bodies, glaring down at me accusatorily.

That was it; I broke into a run right there and then, dashing through the water that came up to my ankles while the rain pelted down on me. I was back on the track within seconds. After stopping for a moment to quickly make sure no vengeful bats were on my tail, I broke into another mad run with my hands over my head in a hopeless attempt to get some cover, wishing desperately for the deluge to stop.

And cursing myself all the way that I should've just taken a chance with the lumberjack killer back at the sawmill.

Chapter Nine

Finally, the rain had stopped, and the harsh midday sun was out again in full force. The wilderness, too, was finally giving way to civilisation. The dirt track ended at a junction with a proper tarmac road complete with lanes and cat's eyes, and I soon spotted a few houses dotting the area, occupying small patches of cleared land amidst the forested backdrop, like little pockmarks on a large swath of green skin.

As I walked along the road, I saw these sparse surroundings lead into a proper, albeit haphazardly planned, housing estate. A perfect example of the settlement's chaotic set-up was the main road, which split off into multiple offshoots, all of which looked to be twisting and turning into their own convoluted paths through the area. Negotiating this maze of a place was going to be difficult, and I began to consider trying my luck knocking on the doors of the houses to get some help. Of course, having a few sympathetic adults standing outside to approach directly would've made things easier for me, but such was my luck that there was no-one around, doing a spot of gardening or sunbathing or whatever it was that people who didn't work in the daytime did outdoors.

I was still drenched from my run in the rain, and my clothes were soaking wet. But fortunately the clothing was in dark colours, so I hopefully wouldn't be attracting too many gawkers once I was among living, breathing people again. I hoped that my clothes would get dry at least by the time I met Michael. If not, he probably would have something mean to say about how I looked. Then again, he'd always be sure to have something mean to say about me, irrespective of whatever state I was in.

Thanks to the six-year age gap between us, my elder brother and I weren't the closest of siblings. For the most part, if Michael wasn't hitting me or calling me names, then he wasn't speaking to me at all. As far as I could remember, he stuck mainly to his room or to the TV whenever he was home, or hogged the computer, boasting that he was chatting to hot girls when he was really just talking to his schoolmates who were just as bored and lame as he was. Sometimes, those deadbeat pals of his would come over, on the pretext of studying in a group. They'd arrive with their shaggy unkempt hair, untucked school uniforms and hideous acne scars, and they'd all either lounge around in Michael's room and laugh together all afternoon in their crude, grunting voices at nothing in particular, or make general nuisances of themselves, strutting around and treating the house like their own private rubbish dump. Certainly, no revision or homework ever got looked at by that bunch, much less completed.

But, to be fair, Michael and I did start speaking to each other a bit more than usual over the last year, and I did manage to have a few normal conversations with him here and there, about football and wrestling and games. In our case, it was probably good enough that we'd been able to reach a point where we could be civil to each other, if not much else.

The closest Michael and I had ever come to really talking like brothers should was when he got turned down by a girl he liked last Christmas. He had gone over to a friend's house party to woo her, dressed like a stooge from a third-rate boy band, right down to sporting a knock-off designer jacket and new trainers and getting his hair lathered in industrial quantities of green jelly. He returned home early, looking like he had been crying all night, and for the next week, he wore only an expression of complete devastation wherever he went. The heartbreak ran so deep that he lost interest in anything fun he liked to do and started getting into all sorts of crazy stuff instead, like attempting to complete his homework on the day of receiving it, a truly disturbing turn of character indeed for my brother.

I helped him get out of this funk, consoling him with the observations that it wouldn't have worked anyway because she was too nice and pretty, and he was too much of an idiot. I also made up a song about Wilbur, the guy who had stolen the girl, Michael's former friend and now-turned love rival:

Wilbur Foo,
Had a poo,
In the loo,
And said ooh ooh!

Sure enough, Michael was back to normal in no time at all, and he even thanked me later by letting me flip through his dirty magazine stash, some copies of which still lay hidden behind jackets of academic texts buried beneath a pile of little-used books in a forgotten corner of his room, out of the reach of our father.

Perhaps he wasn't such a bad guy after all. Even if his negatives – the stealing, the lying, the vandalism, the suspensions, the fights, the smoking, the drinking, the under-age driving – did overwhelmingly outnumber his positives. Mum's departure from our home had hastened Michael's as well, but the same was probably true the other way around; my brother's delinquency had left Mum increasingly distraught, and had only caused my parents to argue more than usual.

It had been so obvious that as the situation got worse with Michael, Mum grew ever so much weaker and wearier, looking like her very life-force was being sapped away by some evil spirit that had latched itself to her. And yet, till the end, until she had left, he had remained her favourite among the four of us. And evidently he still was, judging by how he was getting to speak to her on a regular basis while the rest of us had to wait in the dark, praying for a call that might never come. It would've been an excellent point to put to my mother, but her absence had lasted so long that just getting to talk to her was the only thing on my mind; all other issues could wait in line. Besides, it wasn't anything I wasn't already familiar with; I had long been used to watching others getting favoured treatment over me.

The phone read 12.00. It had been over half an hour since I'd escaped from that truck, and I was nowhere close to getting on a definite course to Badir.

Turning my eyes back to the road, I found, to my dismay, that my current path had doubled back to a junction I had already walked past only a short while ago, thus cancelling out a good five minutes' worth of walking time. Even more frustratingly, the junction had three different roads to follow, and I couldn't tell the errant path from the others, leaving open the possibility of me walking around in circles for who knows how long.

With nothing else to do but press on, I went with my instincts and chose the path whose houses looked most unfamiliar to me. After a little more walking, I came across a large rusted-over rubbish dumpster to my left that I'd not encountered before, and I took this as a sign that I was headed in the right direction and was finally on my way out of there. The dumpster sat by the roadside, in front of a plot of land that might have been in development at some point in the past, but was now teeming with grass and undergrowth and small trees. The front of my shirt immediately went over my nose as I walked by the dumpster, and it stayed there long after the smell of garbage had faded behind me. Houses populated the opposite side of the road, and they looked a lot fancier compared to the ones closer to the wilderness that I'd left behind. These houses weren't just bigger and better but even had fences around them, chain ones at first, and then as I walked on, concrete walls.

But not everything was a pleasant distraction in this neighbourhood, as I soon found out. When I turned the next corner, not too far from the dumpster, I came face to face with a roving pack of feral dogs, which in turn looked straight back at me with a very unhealthy amount of interest. There were three of them, all a mottled mix of black and dark-brown, with docked tails and collarless necks. And they were all huge; the smallest of them on its hind legs would've stood taller than me.

As I took a few slow steps back, they took a few steps forwards, their mouths drooling thick, foamy saliva, and eyes gleaming with raw hunger. Fighting the urge to break into a full-blown run, I tried to maintain a composed retreat, but the hounds persisted, coming towards me with their jaws wide open, showing off jagged canines that glinted like daggers in the sunlight.

Growing increasingly desperate to shake them off, I took a gamble and started backing away a bit faster. This seemed to work at first, and the distance between me and the pack widened. Hoping they were on the verge of giving up the chase, I turned away from them, but then saw two more strays slink in my way, even nastier-looking than the three behind me. A quick dart backwards revealed that those mutts were still on my tail, creeping steadily forwards, their shoulders and knees wound back with starved eagerness. One of them, a dog with half-torn ears and one bulging red eye, let out a long and sinister snarl, and it turned my blood to ice.

The next few moments whizzed by in a flash, and I suddenly found myself squatting on top of the dumpster, trying to keep away from five sets of snapping jaws and praying that they wouldn't be able to jump too high. They were definitely trying hard enough, and a couple of them had almost managed to put their front limbs onto the lid of the dumpster already.

"Help! Somebody help!" I shouted as loudly as I could, jumping away from an attacking dog, the one-eyed one that was determined to make me lunch. I was overcome with an urge to kick at its snout in retaliation, but I stopped myself in time, knowing that to do so would only bring me closer to getting my foot chomped off.

A paw lashed at my side, and I retreated with a whimper, momentary terror setting in. This was met with a series of barks that came at me loud and fiery like gunshots, causing me to recoil further back in instinctive fear. It was remarkable how friendly a couple of them still managed to look, their tongues wagging out of their grinning faces, as if eager to be petted. But not the one-eyed one. No, he was after my blood. He was hopping mad that his prey has escaped his clutches, and he growled murderously and snapped his jaws at me, hoping to set them on my juicy flesh.

Space was limited on top of the dumpster, and keeping still was an impossibility, let alone sitting down and huddling. I had to constantly veer away from the attacks coming in from all sides, doing what I could to avoid getting parts of me torn away and chewed off. My clothes were on the receiving end of a different kind of soaking as I twisted and turned from one angle to another, panic-stricken. I swore to myself that I was never going to get a dog as long as I lived.

Soon, two of the dogs dropped down on all fours, frustrated and seemingly tired, and then, shortly after, two more decided to get some rest. This left behind One-eye as my main opponent. A few rivulets of courage returned when I saw that he was the only one propped up against the dumpster now, and I took my sandals off and clapped them together as near his snout as I dared.

"Go away! Shoo!"

This only made him madder though. He started to snarl viciously, and, with a cry of outrage, made an impressive jump with his forelegs that almost worked in getting him on top of the dumpster with me. The move took me by surprise, and I stumbled and nearly toppled over, prompting two of his friends to run to the other side, where I was about to fall. While I tried to regain my footing, I accidentally dropped one of my sandals to the ground. One-eye wasn't the least bit distracted by it; his eyes didn't leave my face. Angered by the loss of one of my weapons, I waved the remaining one at him even more vigorously.

"Go away! Get out of here!" I cried. One-eye tried to go for my hand rather than surrender.

"Get out! Or I'll ..." My arm drew back; One-eye didn't back down.

"Take that, you son of a bitch!" I hurled the sandal as hard as I could. It missed him completely and hurtled along the road, skipped a few times, then ended up in the grass, inches from the drain. One of the other dogs ran after it, but One-eye wasn't fooled by such tricks. He stepped in closer and engaged me in a face-off, a staring contest that he looked very prepared to fight till the end, even to the point when I'd be a skeleton atop a rubbish container, and he a skeleton in front of it.

This must have been one of the smartest dogs to have ever lived, right up there with Laika and Anubis, a canine criminal mastermind who'd probably put the average Bruneian gangster to shame with his sheer, single-minded viciousness. It was a good thing that he was only interested in messing up rubbish dumps and snacking on little children, or else we'd all be doomed, for he might have just taken over the world.

I paced around a bit on top of the dumpster, the unprotected soles of my feet collecting rust grit, grime and even more unspeakable scraps and specks of crud. The surface was rather hot; though not quite yet scalding, it was uncomfortable enough to stop me from sitting or standing in one place for long. Yet, I was glad that the lid had been closed when I got to it, the alternative I couldn't bear even picturing.

Fortunately for me, I didn't have to wait as long as becoming a skeleton for help to arrive, for only about ten minutes after I had thrown the sandal, my saviours turned up. Unfortunately for me though, they were the most unlikely bunch of saviours I'd have expected, and only a little better than the savage, bloodthirsty hounds at my feet.

Chapter Ten

They came in a white stationwagon that had too many dents and scratches to count and a windscreen displaying what was possibly the world's largest collection of squashed insects and dried bird droppings. Neither the dogs nor I took much notice of the vehicle when it first popped into view a few houses up, motor puttering away and heading down the road in our direction. It was impossible to disregard, however, when it didn't slow down; in fact, it was accelerating steadily, threatening to crash head-on into the dumpster. But at the last moment, it swerved out of the way with a sharp screech of its tyres, barely missing a collision with the pack of mongrels, which were sent scattering about in five different directions.

Instinctively, I flung myself down onto the dumpster's lid and landed on all fours, scraping my shins and bruising my legs. Nevertheless, in the heat of the moment, I felt nothing but unabashed worship for the crazy idiots in the car who'd saved my life, and who'd only just managed to steer the vehicle into the opposite lane, the one the stationwagon should have been using all along, and bring it to a stop.

A group of young men stepped out, one of them with a clean-shaven head, two of them sporting baseball caps, three of them with their hair painted at least two colours, four of them wearing leather jackets over their t-shirts, and all five of them puffing on cigarettes and laughing maniacally amongst themselves. None of them had yet noticed me lying there sprawled on the dumpster.

"Whoahhh ... didya see dat?" giggled the guy with the shaved head, exposing a large gap in between his front two teeth, into which he had stuffed a cigarette. The gap in *Ah Peh*'s teeth was miniscule compared to this guy's.

"Dude!" shrilled his blond companion, slapping the car door repeatedly with his right hand. "Whooooo! That was awesome, man!"

Could it really be? Were these guys the fabled *poklans* I'd heard my classmates talking about? Brunei's very own brand of punks, famous for their love for cigarettes, fast-food burgers, whooping and the creative arts (especially when performed on the walls of public buildings). I had never seen a *poklan* before, but I'd heard a lot about them at school, especially from the teachers, who regarded them as no-good, troublemaking rascals. They were all the rage amongst some of my peers though, who claimed that they were down with these rascals, and who dreamed of living the *poklan*-life of roving around town on lowrider-style cars and blaring out the latest, most slammin' beats while competing with each other to see who could whoop the loudest and the longest. Brunei may have been renowned for its pirates in the past, but here in the present, we had to make do with our *poklans*. My curiosity aroused, I got to my feet and eagerly waited to be acknowledged by them while they giggled and aimlessly walked around their car. I wondered if this was the beginning of a special *poklan* dance.

"Hey! Hey, guys!" I shouted. "Over here!"

At long last, they noticed me.

"Whoahh! Look!" the one with the shaved head sniggered, pointing at me. "What the hell, man?"

I decided to call this one Baldie, obviously only to myself. He had a flame tattoo on the back of his neck, but "Baldie" fit him better than "Mr. Tattoo".

"*Makin kool jua, rumahnya tong sampah*!" one of the other *poklans* collapsed onto his knees in amused laughter, the black cap on his head bobbing up and down with him.

The dogs were long gone, so I jumped down to the road. Standing at ground-level, I was surprised to find that the *poklans* were a lot shorter than they'd seemed at first, and not a great deal taller than me.

"Thanks for saving me! Those dogs were about to kill me, you know," I said, walking towards them.

"*Kuyuk*?" Black Cap expressed his disbelief through his glee. "*Mananya kuyuk*?"

"Hey, bro ... Where're your shoes, man?" asked another *poklan*; he was wearing a thick gold chain around his neck.

"Uh, I threw them at the dogs ..." I pointed to one of my sandals lying by the dumpster. "I really need to get to Badir now. Do you know how to get there? Any chance you could take me?"

This was received with more laughter.

"Hey ... Hey, bro ..." Baldie lurched over, holding his palm out. "Wazzup, man!"

Ah, the universal low-five. This was a promising start. It showed they'd accepted me as one of their own. I extended my hand to touch his.

"Haw haw! Too slow, bro!" But Baldie retracted his hand before I could make contact, and left me swiping at the empty air between us. The rest of the gang hooted even louder as he walked up to my side and wrapped an arm around my shoulder.

"Look, please ..." I tried to shake him off, but Baldie held on to me tightly.

"Bro, we'll take you out, okay? Heehee ... We'll take you someplace fun."

"Uh, no, I need to get to Badir, please ..."

"Dudes! Let's ride!" he yelled, and the other four took this as the signal to frogmarch me to their car.

"Where are we going? Hey, stop it!" I protested, but the gang only doubled up in laughter.

"My sandals!" I cried, pointing desperately to the dumpster, but the *poklans* didn't seem to hear nor care. I was shoved into the backseat of their stationwagon, and then three of them climbed in beside me, trapping me there. The other two got in the front, and we promptly raced off at a speed that I wouldn't have imagined possible for a vehicle this worn out. The sudden force pinned me to the seat, and then a great swerve to the left sent me face-first into the car's door panel, crushing me between its sour, melted-plastic-smelling synthetic padding and Black Cap's right butt cheek.

"Ow! Hey! Be careful!" I screamed. Horrifyingly, my lips had landed inches from a brown smudge that I initially feared to be much, much worse but thankfully turned out to be a mixture of stale anchovy paste and rotting onion fragments.

The car continued to swerve this way and that, and back and forth I went with it, falling against then away from the door's mouldy lining. Elbowing back against Black Cap didn't seem to have any effect on him, but I kept trying anyway. Despite my awkward position, I managed to crane and twist about my neck enough to get myself views of the rest of the car: there were tattered rubber mats on the floor, caked in mud; there were hairs all over them and some other unidentifiable stuff that would have looked at home on a kitty litter tray; there were more brownish stains lining the entire interior of the car, going up almost to its ceiling, along with the odd black scorch marks of cigarettes here and there. And then there was the spacious trunk at the back, of course, bare except for a metal basin and a few black satchels. Now why couldn't they have shoved me in there instead of into the backseat with these three idiots?

"Hey, man! Stop knockin' around! And don't mess wit' the cap, yo!" yelled Black Cap from beside me, finally noticing my repeated elbows into his side. He took off his cap then smoothed over his flattened hair.

"Yeah, dude! *Nanti potong kau punya puchong, ha*!" threatened one of the other *poklans*.

"Eh, dudes, *bising*, eh!" Baldie turned and shouted, ordering us all to pipe down, his eyes very much directed away from the road ahead although he was driving.

"Hey! Where are you taking me? Hey, tell me now!" I yelled at Baldie. The blond guy in the seat next to him switched on the music, drowning me out.

Oooh, bay-beh, bay-beh, you're so freak-ay!

"This is kidnap! You'd better let me go if you're not taking me to Badir!" I tried to scream over the blaring speakers.

Bitches keep tellin' that I come so eaz-ay!

"Do you hear me? Hello!"

Bros from da hood, we like it real sleaz-ay!

"Hey! I'm talking to you!"

Bros like me sho' know we like p ...The car hit a speed bump, and the track was replaced by a series of continuous clicks that sounded a lot better than the song that had been playing. The blond guy banged on the sound system with his fist, but the CD refused to stop clicking. He pushed the eject button in response, and the result was the same.

"Shit, man! It's stuck!"

"Get it out, dude!" snapped Baldie

"I can't, man!"

"Hell wit' dis, I'll sing. Bros like me …" Baldie began, and the others joined in loudly.

I covered my ears and lowered myself to the filth-encrusted floor of the car, pulling my body out of the back-seat squeeze and my head out of the way of Black Cap's ass. I'd ended up being where shit was actually all around me rather than being next to where shit came from, but at least here, I could just about tuck myself into a little ball and wait out this ordeal. If I survived.

The stationwagon continued to swerve and shimmy violently, knocking us around like clothes in a tumble dryer. Each time we went flying to one side, the *poklans* stopped their singing to burst into spontaneous, unbridled guffawing, which only served to alarm me more. During the odd occasion when Baldie drove the car in a straight line, his friends compensated for the lack of movement by rocking together synchronously as they chanted. My car sickness began to surface once more, so I shut my eyes tight and forced all my attention on my eyelids and my hands over my ears.

"You guys are crazy!" I screamed. "Slow down! Slow down! There're other cars on the road!" For the next ten minutes, I remained where I was, while barking out pleas for them to show a bit of sanity. But nothing I said or did seemed to get through to them.

When I finally sensed that the car was moving a bit less chaotically, and had stayed that way for a while now, I dared to open my eyes for a peek out the window. The road here was slightly wider and much straighter than the one I got picked up at, and the traffic was noticeably heavier. This was a good sign; I was finally out of the sticks. But before I could celebrate, the car suddenly turned away from this road and went down a junction that led into another sleepy-looking residential zone.

Large, white houses with blue-tiled roofing and paved-over compounds now lay outside the car windows, along with the occasional smaller wooden shacks that served as convenience stores, barbershops and other assorted small businesses. We drove past them, over a bridge that crossed a large storm drain, and emerged into an area with fewer houses and more open space. To the left was a sight that caused me to shudder: it was a school. To the right was yet another convenience store, albeit one embedded within a proper concrete building that it shared with a few other shops.

We turned in towards this building and came to a stop in front of it, and this was the cue for me to climb off the floor and sit back onto the seat. A stairwell separated the convenience store from an adjacent tailoring outlet, and a neon sign (presently switched off) above the stairwell showed an arrowhead pointing upstairs: "tuition class" and "pool 'n games", the orange plastic tubing of the sign announced. I looked up at the windows of the upper floor but didn't spot anything that could confirm that this claim of fun and education both rolled into one was indeed true. Moreover, I was sure this pool place didn't have anything to do with the one I was trying to reach, so it didn't interest me too much.

I turned my attention to the store. A banner hung over its entrance, declaring it to be privately owned by a certain Mohidin Ali. Its large rolling metal shutters had been neatly folded away to one side like a giant set of curtains, allowing me a good view of the stacks of soft-drink crates and discount shampoo that served as the offers of the day.

"Okay, boy." Baldie was looking at me with the same level of deference one would offer a worm about to be squished flat. "*Nampak tu*? You go in and buy us something, right?"

"What? What do you want me to buy?"

"Glue, *bah*, glue! You know glue? Go! Go in!"

"Why don't you go and buy it yourselves?"

"Dude, just do it, man ..." grumbled Black Cap.

"No. I won't. Why should I?"

Baldie and his cronies looked confused. "We'll make you go!" Black Cap finally said, and the others nodded.

"No, you can't."

Back down I went to the floor, where I latched on to the flap of the front seat's magazine-holder and held tight. Black Cap and the one next to him tried to pull me away but I kept my grip and refused to let go.

"Ha! You can't make me!" I taunted. "You'll have to drag me out with the chair if you want me to leave this car!"

To my surprise, this unnerved the *poklans* rather than enraging them. Baldie's forehead wrinkled up into a network of frown lines, and his eyes narrowed into a pleading squint. "Aw, come on, dude!" he whined. There was a sob of desperation, accompanied by what looked like tears in his eyes. "Come on, help your bros, man!"

"My bros? You guys kidnapped me! I need to be in Badir by this afternoon!" I spat back. "Why am I even here? Why're you asking a kid to get you glue? Just get it yourselves!"

The gang responded with a chorus of moans. "The guy inside

hates us, man! And we need glue for our school projects, man! We'll fail if we don't get it!"

"Yeah, we need to decorate it and shit ..."

"Please, dude, please ..."

"Okay, okay!" I realised this was my chance to make a deal with them. "If I do this, will you guys drive me to Badir? I need to get there and find my brother!"

"No problem, man, no problem!" Baldie offered me a low-five again, but didn't pull away his hand this time.

"Aww, you're awesome, bro!" Black Cap's hands came down on my shoulders to give them a friendly shake.

As I got off the car, I was given ten dollars in the form of six one-dollar notes and a handful of coins, and asked to buy ten bottles of glue. They didn't give me any further instructions; I was simply sent on my way into the shop to purchase the glue they wished to procure. Finding the task easy enough, I went past the paint supplies, power drills and tools to reach the stationery aisle at the back, located behind a shelf of cleaning equipment and bathroom fixtures. But it wasn't only glue I discovered there – I also found myself a treasure trove of shiny black pens, all looking ready to be let loose on fresh, blank sheets of paper. Most of the ink used on the testing pads looked deep and rich, just perfect for signing my next late slip or library fine, or for doing my maths homework.

And that wasn't all. There were blue and red pens on the shelf as well as an assortment of dual, triple and quadruple-coloured ones, the kind I had only seen in the hands of some lucky classmates so far. The only disappointment was the legendary six-coloured pen that was supposed to be able to write in yellow wasn't anywhere to be found. But that wasn't surprising; it *was* a legendary pen after all, and according to Radzi, only one person in Brunei had ever used it, and no-one knew where that person or that pen was now.

There was plenty more in that aisle to be appreciated though: pencil- and ink erasers (existing separately as well as stuck together), compasses, protractors, mechanical pencils, even correction fluid in both pen and brush form. The only thing missing here was a collection of cool pencil cases, especially the kind that came with buttons you could press to make stuff like small sharpeners or magnifying glasses or even little scissors shoot out the sides. The functionality of a Swiss army knife combined with the storage capacity of a child's pencil case was a match made in heaven truly. It was unfortunate, then, that such a thing was unavailable for worship at the moment.

Come to think of it, I did have ten dollars in hand and no-one to check if it all went into getting the glue. Those black pens looked mighty tempting, and the lure of getting a back-up to my G2 began to take hold of me. What if I bought the bottles of glue, and then used the leftover money to buy myself a black pen? I could work something out surely ...

I returned to the bottles of glue. They were small, translucent, plastic ones of about 100 ml capacity and with pink or yellow caps. I picked one up and turned it over in my palm. "Kiko Cat Freinds", it said on the bottle, letter for letter, and a little cartoon ginger cat smiled at me from the top of the cap. I shook about the bottle of greyish-white glue and saw that it had the consistency of a paste, demonstrated by how slowly it shifted to a rapid 90 degree twist of my hand. It wasn't a brand I was familiar with, but it looked like any other glue I'd ever used to make homemade cards and posters.

Sadly, they were a dollar each, and the moment I saw that, something in me deflated. There were no other kinds of glue available at the shop, so if I was going to sneak in a black pen, which were three dollars and fifty each, it would be at the expense of four whole bottles of glue. Could I tell the *poklans* that the store only had six bottles of glue left? Would they believe me? I ran it through my head a couple of times before letting it drift off into that black hole of bad ideas located at the back of my mind. No, I couldn't afford to piss them off. I needed them on my side if I were to get anywhere near Badir, and if that meant sacrificing the chance to get a black pen ... Well, it had to be done.

With a heavy heart, I pulled ten bottles of glue off the shelf and went over to the counter to pay. The guy running the place tallied my purchase then racked up the final price.

"*Mana* you *punya* uniform?" he asked nonchalantly as I handed over the cash.

"Uh, *saya tidak sekolah* ... Uh ..."

"Are you escaping school? Which school do you go to?"

"Well, I ..." Rats, he was on to me. Could he be a truant officer in disguise as a convenience store clerk? If so, I had to hand it to his ingenuity.

"No, no school for me today. I'm sick. Yeah, I ... I've got a cough. Ahem ... bird flu, very contagious. And I need the glue to finish my school project, so thanks and bye!" Without giving the man any time to respond, I grabbed the plastic bag of glue bottles and dashed out of the store to the car. I entered through the rear door, and climbed into the spacious trunk, stumbling over the black satchels as I settled down. My reappearance was met with cheers, and Baldie drove us straight out of there, as if we were escaping in a getaway car after a robbery. But we didn't go very far.

The car zoomed across the road, and into the gateway of the school opposite the convenience store. Baldie slammed down on the accelerator pedal, sending us charging through a lane and into a small parking zone within the compound. From its building and particularly its façade, I determined that it was definitely a government school. The place was almost empty, and unusually so, given that it was 12.30 p.m. and around the time that students would normally start coming out of their classes for lunch.

Baldie took the car to the nearest parking spot available and killed the engine. Then, all the *poklans* turned to me in unison and looked at me with a ravenous hunger in their eyes, and I hurriedly produced the stuff they'd pleaded with me to buy at the store. But I failed to get the grateful reactions I was expecting.

"What the hell, man! Why'd you get these?" Black Cap wailed.

"*Apa ni*!" growled Gold Chain.

"That was all our money, you little shit!"

"Kick your ass and ..."

"Whoa, wait, bros ... We can still use this!" Baldie shushed his fellow *poklans* then informed them calmly that the glue I had bought would indeed work for them.

"Are you sure, dude?"

"You don't remember *masa atu. 'lepas kami* watch movie *di* mall ..."

"*Endless Love Forever*?"

"No! *Middle School Musical, bah*!"

"Oh yeah! *Shiok atu* ..."

"*Nah*! Hey, boy! Give me those bottles!" Baldie said to me with a smile. He was well and truly their leader, looking at how quickly he had managed to calm the others down. While he took the bottles of glue from me, one of his cronies grabbed the basin that was by my side. They proceeded to pour out the contents of all ten bottles into the basin, creating a thick, slimy mass of grey glue that filled about half the container, before throwing most of the empty Kiko Cat bottles to the floor of the car. The five of them then placed the glue-basin on the storage box in between the two front seats, and formed a sort of circle around it, squeezing in together, and leaning over to get their faces as close to it as they could.

"Oh, man! I can feel it! I can feel it!"

"*Shiok, ani*!"

"Oh yeah!"

While the *poklans* went into raptures, I picked up one of the few bottles that had been thrown my way. There was some glue left along the open rim, and I put my nose to it, so I could see what all the fuss was about. It smelt like … glue. Which meant it smelt like nothing at all – just a bit plasticky maybe, but nothing to get so worked up about. Why were these *poklans* getting so excited about glue?

And then it hit me: strange behaviour, crazy hairstyles, weird speech patterns, suicidal driving skills, running around in random villages during school hours … Could these *poklans* be escaped inmates from a mental hospital?

It all finally added up. I strained my mind for relevant references that would help support my theory. Yes, that film we saw on Christmas about a bunch of lunatics who had escaped from an asylum, and then had hijacked a van and gone about terrorising a small town. Their first victim was a kid, too, whom they had lured into their beat-up van with the promise of candy and then devoured alive, saving the boy's fingers and toes for last. Again, it was Kevin's father who had watched it with us, right till the end, in which the local teenage hero managed to draw the lunatics back into the asylum before blowing it up with TNT provided by the sheriff.

"I'm hungry, man ..." Black Cap looked up from the basin suddenly, leering. "I could kill for something right now."

"Heehee! Something fresh!" the blond agreed, smacking his lips together.

I slowly slipped onto the back seat, and then pressed myself against the nearest door and tried to open it; the handle merely rotated around its fulcrum, caught as it was in child-lock mode. Funny; I'd been able to open it freely earlier. Black Cap threw back his head and laughed an incredibly evil laugh, and the others joined in, their maniacal guffaws reverberating throughout the sealed interior of the car and echoing back to me a countless times over. Now I really needed to get out of here.

"Guys, I changed my mind ..." I whispered, gulping down a scream. "Maybe you can just let me out and ..."

"Shut up!" Baldie pulled his head out of the basin, his nostrils streaming with mucus. "Give me those bags." He pointed past my shoulder, and I reached back to grab the satchels for him. I tossed them to him obediently and prayed that the hard, tube-like objects I had felt through their thin, velvety skins weren't explosives.

"Yes!" Baldie cried, pulling out a can of spray paint. I breathed a sigh of relief. "Right, dudes! Let's finish trashing the school! Whooooooo!"

They threw their heads back in unison to make a high-pitched whoop, and then they exited the stationwagon together, taking the canisters with them, and leaving me inside.

I was free.

Just like that, huh? I watched them disappear into the school, and once I was sure they were gone, I stepped out of one of the doors they had left open.

As I walked away from the stationwagon, I saw that cars were trickling in now, and parents and drivers were gathering in a sheltered seating area near the parking zone while students started to emerge from the school's building. There was no-one around who looked like he or she might be a member of the school's staff, so I ducked my head and started walking away briskly from the stationwagon. The gate seemed painfully distant, and I was set for yet another long, nerve-wracking walk.

The dark clouds from the morning had fully left the sky, and the sun was at its brightest, baking the road and the grass and my bare feet, and bringing out an unbearable glare on anything with a reflective surface. Waves of heat spiralled up and danced in front of me, and as I neared the gate, suddenly, a smoky screen appeared in the distance, and featured on it was a snooker den, superimposing itself over the convenience store I had purchased the glue from. This was definitely the den that Michael would be in that afternoon; a sign stood next to it, magically magnified a hundred times over, and it announced "Michael is here".

I was heading towards the den when I heard a great roar from behind me; it brought me out of this daze. I turned around to see the *poklans* fleeing the school. An infuriated man in a red shirt and a *songkok* was in hot pursuit of the gang, his ample flab flapping about him like wings. Two other men were running towards the *poklans* from the opposite direction, to cut off their way to their car. It worked, and they were forced to change course, turning away from the stationwagon. The angry fat-man also turned around to follow them, providing me with a view of the back of his shirt, which I saw had been painted white. There was another patch of paint on the seat of his otherwise dark trousers, and trails of white were trickling down his legs and to the ground as he ran about. The other two pursuers followed him, in turn, and before long, all of them were out of sight, disappearing into the school's building.

I carried on my way, forcing my legs to move faster. It wasn't just that I was worried about getting implicated in whatever crimes the *poklans* had committed; I also felt uneasy hanging around in a school area without having on my uniform or proper footwear. I'd already roused the shopkeeper's suspicions; I didn't want any more concerned adults checking up on me. Pa occasionally spoke of the truant police snatching up kids wandering around on their own during school hours; even if there weren't any of those goons already watching me, it would surely be only a matter of time before any of the regular grownups here turned me in for not being in school like a good little boy. And then I'd be sent to the jail disobeying kids were sent to, which would be exactly like school except there'd be no holidays at all for ten years and the guards would double as my teachers, and give me punishments ten times worse than the ones Mrs. Yap gave us; I might have to squat under my desk for a hundred and fifty minutes in jail instead of the fifteen minutes I did at school.

And obviously Pa would find out about it, so I'd have no choice but to spend the rest of my life repeating the fifth grade over and over again in prison, until I died, because even that would be better than facing him with my criminal charges.

I moved on to thinking about what my next move should be. Any move would suffice, so long as it got me closer to Badir without getting me closer to death at the same time. Hitchhiking? Walking? There was little that I could hope to accomplish on my own when I still didn't know where I was, let alone how to get myself to Badir.

The phone! Of course, Kevin's phone!

Thank goodness the *poklans* had never thought to rob me. I took it out of my pocket and brought up the contacts list. Calling my cousin or even my sister for help were possibilities, but I wasn't sure if they'd be of much use. They'd likely be tied up with their funeral jobs anyway, and there was also the chance that one of the adults might answer instead of them.

Radzi the know-it-all it had to be, then. Also, Radzi the reliable, who answered exactly on the third ring, a habit he'd maintained with remarkable consistency for as long as I'd known him. He patiently listened to the tale of my ill-fated quest, and then observed quite wisely that it wasn't in my character to make exaggerations of this scale, and thus decided that I was telling the truth, however outlandish my story was. He wasn't quite the know-it-all when it came to giving me useful advice though.

"I don't know, man … You don't even know where you are …"

"I'm counting on you, Radzi! Don't you have anything to give me?"

"Yeah, well, there are a lot of schools in Brunei. Saying you're at one isn't much help. Why don't you look for a sign with the school name? Can't you see one?"

Why hadn't I thought of that before calling him?

I had just cleared the main gate, so I turned back to see if I could find any indication of the school's name. There was a concrete wall stretching across the front of the school compound, at the centre of which, and immediately next to the main gate, was the school's official mural, a gigantic open book lying open in front of a burning torch. At the top of this painting were the words "WELCOME TO", and at the bottom was the word "*SEKOLAH*" – and that was all I could see of the school's name. The rest of it lay buried under a splodge of paint over which were drawn a series of random figures.

"I can't see the name. Someone's painted some crap over it."

"Well, try looking closer."

I approached the wall with some apprehension, desperate to not draw too much attention to myself. "Let's see ..."

On closer inspection, I found that the crap drawn there were six cartoons, standing side-by-side with arms draped around each others' shoulders, their faces stunningly rendered in such lifelike detail that I found it hard to imagine that this had been done with just spray paint. Why, five of them were the spitting image of the *poklans* who had abducted me, to the extent that actual "wanted" photos might not have looked as real. Inexplicably, a figure best described as a human-sized banana wearing a leather jacket and a pair of sunglasses stood next to them, while the *poklans* themselves were depicted with regular-sized bananas sticking out of their trouser pockets. To top it off, an inscription painted below the image said "*Pisang Panas* Gang".

The "Hot Banana" gang, eh? I was sure nobody with an ounce of sanity would want any of their bananas. They could keep them to themselves, and share them with each other for all I cared.

"Have you ever heard of the *Pisang Panas* Gang?" I said into the phone.

"What the hell is that?"

"Never mind ... I don't see any name anywhere."

"What about by the road? No signs there?"

Radzi waited while I trudged to the nearest pedestrian crossing. All it had was the customary "slow down" notice; the school's name was nowhere to be found on it.

"Nope."

"Why don't you ask one of the parents? Just pretend you're visiting a friend or a cousin."

"No way, I'm not taking that risk. Besides, I'm way out of there already. I can't go back in again!"

"Well, has the phone got internet? You could check, but I don't think ..."

"What could I search for without the name of the school? There's nothing else around here but a small shop."

"What kind of shop?"

"You know, one of those *kedai runcit*. Nothing major. Owned by some guy called Mohidin."

"Mohidin? Wait, are you sure?"

"Why?"

"I've got a cousin called Mohidin. He's got a small shop near Kampung Daun and it's supposed to be next to a school."

"Really? Could this be his shop then?"

"Maybe."

"What does your cousin look like?"

"He's in his twenties ... He's thin, has some acne scars ..."

"It does sound like him," I said excitedly. "Great, I can hand the phone over to him then, and you can tell him to help me out."

Radzi was silent. "Hello? You there? Hello?"

Still no response. I took the phone off my ear and glanced at its screen: blank as an exercise book on the first day of school.

My repeated attempts to restart the device didn't work, and I had to stop myself from throwing the useless thing onto the pavement and smashing it into pieces. All that hope built up only for this to happen? Could nothing go right today? I didn't even get to ask Radzi where exactly Kampung Daun was, or how far it was from Badir.

I wondered if this man Mohidin would agree to help me after a mere mentioning of his cousin's name. There was little else I could do but try my luck. After all, so far, I'd survived a ride in a coffin, a cursed house, a horde of bats, a pack of wild dogs, and a gang of lunatics. How much worse could a simple storekeeper be?

Chapter Eleven

It turned out that Mohidin wasn't so terrible after all. He listened to me attentively, although with a blank face that didn't give away any emotion, as I basted my story with layer upon layer of acts of filial piety and noble self-sacrifice. I told him of my intention to find Michael and left out the parts about using my brother to try and get a hold of my mother, focusing instead on how he had been *Ah Kong*'s favourite grandson and that it was my sworn duty to bring him back for the funeral. I didn't really know why I hadn't wanted to tell Mohidin the real reason behind my wanting to find Michael, especially since my quest to find out the truth about my mother was just as worthy.

"What a story ..." he finally said.

"Yes ... Yes, it is," I nodded solemnly.

"Your mother and then your brother and then your grandfather ... All gone."

"Of cour ... Oh, right, yeah ..." For a moment, I thought he was referring to my heroic encounters with the dogs and the *poklans*. "Yeah, all that too ..."

"And you are here by yourself ..."

"Yup! Well, thanks partly to Radzi."

"Radzi ..."

The shopkeeper's vacant look betrayed nothing. His face remained blank, and I could not glean anything from the flattened tone of his voice either; it was a different sort of "flat" from my father's voice, who tended to sound flat from being fed up all the time. Mohidin just sounded and looked emotionless. Radzi certainly hadn't got to that part of his description (even if whatever little he'd managed to tell me about his cousin did fit, especially the acne).

Mohidin's English was practically perfect though, much like Radzi's, and once one got past the monotony of his voice, one would realise that the grammar and diction were spot-on, and that he enunciated his words with minimal hesitation or stutter. Other pieces of soft evidence that tied him to my good friend? His accent also had a mild American twang to it, again, similar to Radzi's (though this in itself wasn't too uncommon amongst Bruneian youths in general).

"Um, he said you'd be able to help me …"

"Did he?"

"Er, yeah … He said you were a great guy. His favourite relative. The best shopkeeper in Kampung Daun!"

Mohidin gave a disbelieving look in response to my flattery.

"Boy, what I should do is take you home …"

I began to panic. This was the last thing I needed: one man's good intentions ruining my last hope of success.

"Oh no, you can't! You've got to help me find my brother! If you take me back, then everything will stay the way it is and nothing will ever get better!" I knew I was babbling, but I had to throw whatever I could at him, no matter how desperate it made me look.

"I should take you back. It's not safe for you to run around like this."

"Well, if you're worried about me being by myself, you could come along. To Badir. It won't be a problem, and I promise it wouldn't take too long."

He paused to contemplate my offer. "You really need to do this? It's that important?"

"It's very, very important. Oh, please ... I know deep down that it would make my whole family so very, very happy when we're all together again."

"And if I said no?"

"Well ... I'd find some other way of getting there then," I said. "I need to find my brother, and I need to get him to the funeral, so he can see our grandfather one last time. And I need to help him reunite with our family. No matter what, I can't give up now." My best efforts at displaying strong and unshakable love for my brother probably didn't come across half as well as I wanted it to, but it was the best I could manage. "I'd do anything to find my brother. I'd sneak into a car, I'd run, I'd even ... I'd even go to a *bomoh,* if I knew where to look. It was my grandfather's dying wish, after all ..."

That last bit was the cherry on the cake. Mohidin raised an eyebrow and then leaned back in his chair, his hands clasped in front of his chest. His short and flat hair exposed a vast, protuberant forehead, and beneath it, a pair of dark brown eyes, which were wide open now.

"Okay, boy ..." he relented finally. "Wait here." He left his seat, going past me and heading through a door next to his counter, shutting it behind him. Intrigued, I approached it, regardless of his instruction to stay put, and placed an ear near its handle to eavesdrop. I could make out the faint sounds of him speaking to someone. Was he discussing my problem with someone over the phone? Could it be Radzi?

He suddenly stopped talking, and then I detected the sound of footsteps walking towards the door. I didn't want to get caught snooping red-handed, so I scuttled out of the way, managing to re-assume my original position in the chair just as Mohidin opened the door and stepped out of the side room.

"Okay, boy," he said assuredly. "I'll help you."

"Really? That's great."

That was rather quick. Almost too quick. But nothing seemed amiss otherwise, so I was only too happy I'd stumbled upon this opportunity, and I put aside all those things I'd been taught about stranger-danger (technically, he wasn't even a stranger, since he was Radzi's relative). Besides, the fact that he had initially refused my request and threatened to take me home first was enough proof that he was a normal, sensible and perfectly dependable adult.

"We should go now, if you want to catch your brother on time. Can you help me close the shop?"

That I did by helping him pull the metal shutter at the shop's entrance across its track until it was fully extended. I then watched as he secured the padlock and put up a "closed" sign before leading me to his ride, a white saloon car. With everything taken care of, we set off for Badir, me sitting in the front passenger seat of a car for the first time in more than a year.

I allowed myself to sit back and relax a little. The radio was on, and a dance anthem with a repetitive jackhammer-like beat and with lyrics that consisted solely of the words "ass" and "tap" blared out from the car's speakers as we drove down the long coastal highway. The road was not as close to the sea as to give me a view of the shoreline though; rather, there was nothing but forest on both sides of the car. Stretches of trees filled up the view outside our windows, keeping up with us almost as closely as the ever-present sun in the sky. It may have been everywhere, and it all looked the same, but it was still my favourite sight to see whenever I was in a car. My sole quibble, minor as it was, was with our driving speed. The clock showed 1.10. It was already fifteen minutes since we'd left the shop, so I asked Mohidin to step it up a bit.

"Sorry, I can't go faster. This road is quite dangerous. Too much overtaking. Some students died here last week."

"The story that was in the newspapers? The one that said that one of them was cut in half?"

"Yes, that's the one. Sad, isn't it?" Mohidin said, yawning. "Have you eaten yet? Are you hungry? Thirsty?"

"Oh, that's alright. I had breakfast this morning, and I'm not that hungry now." Honestly, I was growing rather hungry, but I felt too shy to trouble Mohidin with a request for refreshments. He was already doing me a massive favour by driving me to Badir, not to mention kindly lending me a fresh pair of sandals to replace the ones I'd lost back at the dumpster, so asking for something else from him felt like going too far.

"You must have some lunch. A growing boy like you … No wonder you're so thin." Mohidin pointed to the back seat.

"I don't have any food right now, but there's a bottle of water there, if you'd like," he offered.

I turned around to look at the half-full bottle of mineral water on the seat bobbing along to the car's motion. Any feelings of thirst I might have had rapidly evaporated away though when I spotted a strange-looking black plastic bag sitting beside it. A small, familiar-looking piece of red cloth stuck out of it, and whatever else was inside filled it out well enough to make the bag bulge into the shape of a pumpkin.

"Do you really run the store by yourself? It must be hard …" I asked, turning away. I really wanted to ask him about the bag and what was in it, but decided not to.

"It's okay."

"I mean, the type of people you must get … Like those dreadful *poklans* who forced me to buy glue from you."

"The ones who take things without paying are worse. But you can't stop it."

"That's awful! Do you get a lot of that?"

"More than enough. Too many kids playing pool upstairs; when they get bored, they come down and hang around my shop, then run off with things without paying."

"I see … But, hey, it must still be pretty cool owning your own business. And to own one when you're so young."

"I'm not so young." Most would have said this with a smirk or a grin, but Mohidin did it as blandly as one possibly could. "The shop went to me after my parents died."

"Oh … When did your parents pass away?"

"Soon after my brother. It was my family's time then … Like how it's your family's time now."

I couldn't really argue with that. "It must've been hard …"

"Yes, but Tok Dodol says not to dwell on the past. People must always to look to the future."

"How did they?"

"They had … accidents."

"Oh … Hey, Mohidin, who's Tok Dodol?"

"He's the one I asked for advice about helping you."

"He was in that room?"

"No, but I can reach him anywhere. I can even talk to him in my head."

I felt my throat growing dry. He couldn't really be serious about this whole friend-in-my-head thing … Could he?

"Tok Dodol told me he saw you coming. A boy with a good heart who wants to help his family."

I couldn't believe what I was hearing.

"A person like you deserves help. So I had to help. It's the right thing to do."

"Thanks, that's nice but, who is he?"

"He is Tok Dodol."

"Yeah, but …"

"He keeps me safe. Do you want to see him, boy?"

"Um …" No, thanks, I'd rather not.

"He is here."

"Here? Like, in this car?"

"Yes."

I gave the car's interior a thorough scan. "I don't see anything …"

"He's in there." Mohidin pointed at the glove compartment in front of me. My eyes darted to the closed door.

"Open it and see."

"Ah." I'd really rather not.

"Don't be scared. Go ahead."

I kept my hands firmly by my side. Mohidin drove on, saying nothing further in return, yet silently pressing upon me the burden of opening the glove box and finding out for myself about Tok Dodol.

"Isn't it a bit too small for a person?"

"Just open it and see," he droned again.

Well, what was the worst that could happen? Haltingly, I

reached out and wrapped my fingers around the handle of the compartment's door. I held my breath as I pulled: the latch clicked, and the door creaked open. Initially it was all dark inside, but as I kept pulling, an automatic light was triggered on, and then I could see what Mohidin was so eager to show me.

I jumped back a bit, recoiling with genuine dread. There was a small object lying there, covered by a brown sackcloth and surrounded by a loose scattering of fine soil that was spread across the floor of the compartment. Some tendril-like things that looked to be coming from the back of the object ran curled and twisted over the soil, resembling dried-up roots coming off the bottom of a plant. And then there was the blood. Bright red and fresh-looking blood, drawn in a weird circular pattern over the surface of the sackcloth, with three pins sticking out of it that made it look as if the bag was bleeding from three separate stab wounds.

"Do you see?" Blasé as ever, Mohidin kept his eyes on the road as he asked for my opinion on his secret adviser.

"Yeah. I see." Given the many terrifying events I had experienced that day, I was near exhaustion, and too weary to generate the horror that this situation would (and should) have normally commanded.

"Is that real blood?" Perhaps if I kept him talking, we could carry on doing so till the completion of my quest, and he'd never get a chance to use me for a ritual human sacrifice.

"Yes."

"Where did you get it?"

"It's mine."

I sat there, speechless and immobile, awaiting the next move by Mohidin. He could have come at me with a hatchet and a clown mask on, and I wouldn't have had the senses to do anything about it.

"He's my only friend. The only one who cares about me."

That snapped me out of it. "Really? You don't have any other friends?" Anything to keep his mind on the conversation and off any potential thoughts to do something unsavoury to the boy travelling in the car with him.

"No, I don't. Nobody's ever interested in talking to me. I'm just the guy in the background, wherever I am. But that's alright." He followed this up with a smile, the first one I'd seen since I had met him. But it was not a real smile, and not one made from genuine happiness. Adults rarely ever smiled at me while truly meaning it, so I could usually tell when a smile was fake or not, and this was about as fake as it got.

But while those false smiles usually annoyed me, Mohidin's only made me feel sorry for him. His upturned lips made a very poor cover for all the loneliness I could see written over the rest of his face.

"Why don't they want to talk to you? You seem like a nice guy."

His smile grew bigger, and it looked as if he was genuinely touched by my remark. Maybe I'd misjudged him; how could someone this pitiful ever do anything harmful, at least intentionally. "I don't know ..." he mumbled. "Anyway, it doesn't matter."

I knew, and it did matter. Exuding all the warmth and compassion in the world wasn't quite enough to cancel out the weird vibe that he was giving off at the same time.

Wasn't he on good terms with his cousin? Maybe he wasn't counting relatives as friends. I'd have to speak about this with Radzi later, and maybe even discuss with him about how we could get Mohidin to act less ... freaky. But in the meantime, I decided that it wouldn't hurt to be nicer to him.

"Hey, er, I'll be your friend," I offered. "It was really sweet of you to help me, and I'd do anything to pay you back, but my friendship is all I have at the moment."

"Thank you," he replied, still smiling. "I accept you as my friend. Tok Dodol always accepts people with good hearts."

At any rate, if Mohidin did intend to kill me, it would've been much easier to bump me off back at the store, where he wouldn't need to concentrate on driving at the same time, or worry about witnesses. But he hadn't done anything bad at the most opportune time for him, and this probably meant that he could be trusted after all.

Also, I was probably blowing the whole Tok Dodol issue out of proportion. *Bomohs* like the Malacca Lady, whom *Ah Em* liked to consult, did this sort of thing all the time, and people paid them money for it. I was much better off than those regular patrons of invoked spirits then, seeing as I was getting actual help from one rather than just wishy-washy blessings. Mohidin hadn't solicited a fee for his aid either, not that I was sure if he was a *bomoh* himself.

Of course, it was still quite unnerving sitting in front of that bloody thing with all those pins sticking out of it.

"Let me tell you a story," Mohidin began in a low voice when he caught me sneaking a look at the glove box. "A story about a young boy like you. A boy with parents and a brother who went to school like all children do." Mohidin had stopped smiling now.

"But the children at school didn't think he was normal. They didn't want to be friends with him, and they bullied him and called him names, until the day he couldn't stand it anymore and changed schools. But it was always the same wherever he went.

"You see, this boy was born with a lump on his neck. This lump was big enough that he couldn't hide it from his classmates, and because his parents were poor and had little schooling, he'd never seen a doctor about it. So it kept growing and growing, and the other children kept pointing and laughing, and the teachers just kept quiet. It was as if the boy didn't exist to them.

"Because he didn't have any real friends, the boy had to make them up in his head. And he made up as many friends as he could ever want, and these friends never made fun of him nor called him nasty things. They were under his control, and they couldn't do anything unless he wanted them to. These friends were good to the boy, all of them, and took good care of him.

"But one of them was especially good to the boy.

"This one friend told him one day, 'tomorrow, a wonderful thing will happen, and your life will change forever'. And you know what happened? The next day, while crossing a road, a car knocked him down. He wasn't hurt badly, but the lump bled and bled, and it fell off him by itself.

"And everything did change from that day onwards. At school, his classmates were suddenly nice to him. Teachers began to see him like any other child now. Everything turned out truly wonderful, and all the friends in his head celebrated. That one special friend, whose prediction had come true, was very happy too for the boy.

"The boy was very grateful to this special friend. So grateful that he felt he needed to pay him back. He knew that it had to be something valuable, but not expensive because he had no money to spend.

"After some thinking, he finally knew what he could give his friend ..."

Mohidin stopped his tale abruptly to swerve the car to avoid a speeding overtaker. While he complained about how careless driving was becoming the norm on Bruneian roads these days, I closed shut the glove compartment. Not particularly keen on hearing the end of his story, I diverted his attention further by enquiring about his past vehicular mishaps and near-misses. Hopefully, the yarn he had just shared with me was the absolute pinnacle of his weirdness ...

By now we'd long since left the highway, and directly ahead of us was the last obstacle to our destination: a traffic jam that was clogging up a huge, three-lane roundabout with five exits and no traffic lights. According to Pa and *Ah Peh*, such congestion was a daily nationwide problem largely caused by the lunch-hour rush of civil servants scrambling from their offices to various schools around the capital, dashing to get themselves and their children home as quickly as possible. This current jam was as bad a jam as any other I'd ever experienced, and I had plenty of experience getting caught up in them because my school was not too far away from here.

Getting onto the roundabout was the worst part; it felt as if we were playing a game of dare with the oncoming cars, which kept trying to cut into our path, a game where the results were either victory or a car crash. Fortunately, Mohidin played this game well and pulled us away smoothly into the circular flow of vehicles and then into the second exit, straight for Badir.

But then, it was time for another setback. After we had cleared the roundabout, we were faced with a horde of cars and vans and trucks of all shapes and sizes vying to fill every single parking slot in sight, like endless streams of ants swarming over each other in a mad scramble for a dropped sweet. We were stuck properly this time, and there were no tricks that were going to get us out of this one quickly.

With our car forced to a standstill, I had nothing much else to do but look outside to pass the time. The lane that our car was trapped in ran alongside a row of shops, and the most popular one amongst them, and situated just outside my window, was a fast-food outlet that specialised in fried chicken. I stared at the pictures on the shop's glass walls, of golden-brown, deep-fried and battered chicken parts nestled on beds of fluffy turmeric rice. Customers were lined up outside the shop, the queue extending from the entrance and along the common walkway, and including everyone from executives in business suits to builders in dusty overalls. Saliva started to pool in the floor of my mouth, and I forced myself to look away to something else before my stomach got a chance to have its say.

No, there was no time to get sidetracked, even for lunch. Also, it still felt wrong to trouble Mohidin for food. I thought of the disapproving scowl Pa would give me for the dishonour I'd bring myself and the family by begging a stranger for a meal; that was enough to placate my pangs for the time being.

I turned my attention instead to an empty DVD and video game store next door to the chicken outlet, and then to an almost empty mobile phone dealership, and then to a pretty empty sports shop and finally a very full $5 discount outlet. My eyes ran over the adverts that seemed to pepper the entire block, coating the walls and the pillars with promises of every kind of deal imaginable: "Thai massage with cut/wash"; "Japanese/Korean/Mandarin tutor for hire"; "free mobile phone/DVD crack". It was surprising that I couldn't find anyone selling parking spaces to the highest bidder here; now that kind of a deal would've definitely brought in loads of customers, including us.

It took a full twenty minutes before Mohidin was finally forced to settle for a tight squeeze between two SUVs, under the full glare of the midday sun and next to a rubbish collection point. The dumpsite was a white concrete hut without a proper door, into which a considerable quantity of garbage had already been deposited, most of it spilling out of their black bags and onto the heavily-stained tiled floor. In spite of sitting behind closed doors and windows, I could smell the rancid stench from the dump that was somehow seeping into the car.

"So, boy, do you know where we're going?" Mohidin asked.

"Friendly Garden Pool Centre. Uh, the address is ..." Oh no, I couldn't remember it. My brain had picked the worst time to forget something. Moreover, my eyes were unhelpfully getting distracted by a stray dog with a very prominent set of udders, which was snoozing underneath one of the SUVs parked nearby, seemingly unperturbed by the unwholesome air it was breathing. Was it really fast asleep? Or was it simply pretending to, while waiting for a chance to attack when I least expected it? These things were everywhere nowadays; was there some kind of national canine conspiracy to turn me into doggie chow?

"Wait, let me ... hmm ..." I said as calmly as I could, shaking off my thoughts about the dog.

"Okay, let's try asking in there," Mohidin pointed to a big department store that stood opposite to the rubbish dump, only about ten metres away. We had parked near the rear part of the store, so we'd have to walk over to the front to get in.

"I didn't forget it. Just let me think ..."

"Come on, you don't have much time. You're late as it is." We left the car, holding our breaths as we walked past the dumpsite and towards the store's entrance.

In Brunei, they sometimes forgot to tarmac the smaller roads that went around the shops, and this was one such road. Through my new sandals, I felt the jagged, pebbly surface of the path with each step. Also, the road was baking hot. How that bitch could lie there so comfortably under that car was anyone's guess; I couldn't imagine it being that much cooler down there. Perhaps all these strays had superhuman, or rather super-doggie, powers, honed through a life on the rough side of town; for instance, One-eye's superpower was his super intelligence and this one's was heat resistance. It wouldn't be long before they indeed took over the world.

With no pavements or walkways leading into the store from its rear, and to avoid getting in the way of oncoming cars, Mohidin and I scurried quickly over the grilled coverings of the drains that ran alongside the building, squeezing ourselves between the parked vehicles and the side wall of the store. Not making our ordeal any easier were a) the stink rising up from the drains and b) the patches of bluish-green sludge that coated the grilles so extensively that landing on one at least every other step was unavoidable.

Even so, we soon reached the department store's entrance, which, with its shutters well hidden, looked simply like a large hole in the building's wall. As far as I could see, no-one was entering or leaving the store. A man who looked like the world's oldest security guard sat by its entrance, snoozing away on a plastic chair, dressed in a red beret and crumpled khaki fatigues, a foot-long wizard-like white beard lying against his chest. An unmanned soft-ice cream dispenser sat forlornly next to him like a mechanical grandchild desperate for attention, its orange, green and pink buttons so bright with deluded optimism and so close to being able to distract one away from the rust marks and cobwebs that had gathered around the rest of its neglected body. The security guard didn't stir awake as we walked in.

The store's inside was similarly subdued, but not unexpectedly so, given the time of day. Upon entering, we saw to our left a pharmacy and traditional medicine counter, while straight ahead was a mobile-phone-and-accessories stand as well as the escalator leading to the first floor. To our right were rows of checkout lanes, and beyond these lanes was the groceries section, where I saw a couple of old ladies pushing along their shopping carts, wandering from the vegetables to the dairy aisle in time to the slow sax music being played through the loudspeakers.

We decided to try the pharmacy counter, which was a single glass-casing staffed by a bespectacled middle-aged woman, sitting cross-legged and reading a newspaper. The wares on display were a mix of Western medicines and traditional remedies; I could see many bottles of ginseng as well as other dried-up herbal stuff I didn't know the names of.

"Uh, excuse me?" I walked over to the woman while Mohidin stayed back, watching.

"Hmm? What?" She barely managed to tear herself away from her paper, and peered over her glasses to flash me an annoyed look.

"Uh, do you know where the Friendly Garden ..."

"The what? I can't hear you!"

"The Friendly Garden Pool Centre!" I shouted.

"No. I don't know. Don't shout at me, boy! And why are you dressed like that? You look like you're going to a funeral!" She then returned to her paper.

I slunk away from her and looked to Mohidin, who only shrugged in response. I pleaded with my eyes and tried to convey how much I wanted him to step in and try asking her. Or at least scold her for acting so nasty to me. It came as a pleasant surprise when he did respond to my silent cry for help. Any other adult I knew, and especially my father, would've walked away from there, and would've scolded me instead.

"Can I have one box of Vitamin C tablets? And some cough syrup? Also, my nose is a bit itchy. Could I have some of that, uh, hay fever medicine?"

This wasn't really going the way I had expected it to.

"Medicine?" the woman snapped. "Do you have a prescription for that?" The woman gave Mohidin the same menacing once-over she'd given me from behind her glasses.

"Huh? But I usually get all this at ..."

"There's no registered pharmacist here now. She is the only one who can make the sale for these medicines."

"When is she coming back?"

"How should I know?" The woman looked repulsed for some reason.

"But ..."

"Here, take your vitamins. That's all I can give you right now. That comes up to twenty-five dollars and eighty cents."

"It costs that much? But ..."

"Check the price before you come up to the counter next time," she cawed. Mohidin opened his wallet and slowly, and very reluctantly, began pulling out a couple of notes. Looking defeated, my companion handed over the money and took his bag of vitamins without so much as a snarky word back at her.

He then beat a hasty retreat, and I was compelled to follow him out of the building.

"Why'd you let her talk to you like that? I mean, aren't you an adult too? You can't let yourself get treated like that by her."

"Ah, never mind," he muttered, stopping in front of the dozing guard and looking down glumly at the contents of his plastic bag. "It's not worth it."

"That woman's so mean. She must be related to my teacher, Mrs. Yap. One day, I'll get her arrested for crimes against humanity!"

"Boy, when you grow up ..." He left the sentence hanging.

"When I grow up, what?"

He sighed. "Nothing. Do you know the address of the pool centre? The *simpang*? You're already twenty minutes late."

"Ah, crap. Wait, I ..." How I wished I'd written it down somewhere. "Let's see ... *Simpang* 46? 36?"

"Well, this is *Simpang* 68 right here," Mohidin pointed to a sign nearby. "Are you sure about the number?"

"Hey, wait, it's 64! *Simpang* 64! We can't be far away! Let's go back in and ask where *Simpang* 64 is!"

"We'll go somewhere else," Mohidin said with a small voice and darted a helpless look at the woman at the pharmacy. I accompanied him as he walked across the street to another block, hopefully one populated by a less hostile set of shop workers.

We were in luck at the next place we tried. It was a stationery shop manned by a beaming Filipino, who immediately pointed out the way for us without any hesitation. I felt like reciprocating his kindness by purchasing something for his troubles, but unfortunately, I didn't have any money, and it felt so wrong getting Mohidin to do it on my behalf. In any case, nothing on the newsstand grabbed my interest, and the comics I usually browsed through at shops like this weren't stocked here. Nothing piqued Mohidin's fancy either, so the most we could do was thank the man, which we did profusely and gratefully before following his directions to *Simpang* 64.

Our destination turned out to be a rather isolated part of Badir town. There was a single block of shops here, formed of six individual units lined side by side, and the only one with a sign or banner of any sort happened to be the Friendly Garden Pool Centre, the second unit from the far end of the building.

Three of the other units were locked up, and were probably out of business. The one at this end was occupied by a tyre dealership, and the unit next to it was a coffee-shop with an interior so badly-lit and grimy that it looked like it was last refurbished about fifty years ago. The place however couldn't have been more than ten years old, because that was about the age of Badir itself – before that, this whole area was nothing but swampland. Neither the tyre dealer nor the café looked like they had any customers at the moment; the café seemed completely deserted, while the tyre dealership was filled with stacks of heaped-up tyres and various car parts that prevented me from making out if there was any activity inside. It felt refreshing to be out of the way of all the cars and the bustle though; the noises coming off the busier roads nearby were reduced here to a mild background hum and a few muted horn-honks.

As we walked up to the pool centre, I tried to look through its glass façade that was plastered over with advertisements for new mobile-phone subscription services and fast food joints, and managed to get a heavily-obscured glimpse of a row of computer terminals, but saw no pool tables. A handwritten sign pasted awkwardly between a few ads proclaimed that no-one in a school uniform would be allowed entry into the pool centre, and that smoking wasn't allowed within the business premises.

As I pushed open the door, Mohidin made a move to walk in first. "Uh, Mohidin? Can I go in by myself?" I asked, holding open the door.

"What? No, I can't let you do that."

"Well, it's my brother ... He might get a bit jittery if he sees me with you. He's so stupid that he might think you're an undercover police officer or something. It's probably better if it's just me."

Again, I didn't know why I felt so strongly about hiding the fact that this whole thing was really about my desire to speak to my mother, and learning what Michael knew that I didn't about her. It was not like Mohidin would've laughed or called me a weakling; he of all people would've understood. Yet, I didn't feel too sure about confiding in him.

"I don't know ..."

"Please?" I begged him. "You trusted me enough to bring me here ... Just trust me enough for this too."

Mohidin gave the pool centre an unsure look, his eyes running up and down its walls. "Well, to be honest, I've seen children younger than you go into places like this ... But after ten minutes, I'm coming in if you haven't already come out."

"Okay. But I am sure I'll be back before that."

In truth, I wasn't sure about anything. Smiling at Mohidin so as to set his mind at ease, I took a deep breath and hurried into the pool centre. I was almost half an hour late and had no idea about what I'd say to convince Michael to come back home. If he was still here, that is.

Chapter Twelve

One quick breath in, and I was ready to race back out. Or at least get down on all fours and make the rest of my way in crawling. A dense fog of tobacco smoke filled the room, and my throat started to hack while my eyes watered. Clearly, I was in a lair of *poklans*. And to become a *poklan* probably meant being able to develop a natural tolerance to, or even survive on, pollutants and toxic waste. Or perhaps it was the other way around? Maybe this was what mutated people into *poklans* in the first place and if that was the case, then I'd better hurry up. The last thing I wanted was to get turned into one.

It took a few more moments before I was able to clear my eyes and take in my surroundings: I saw a gloomy room with ten computer terminals but no pool tables. Two customers were clicking away at these terminals creating noisy explosions on their screens, and contrary to the sign outside, they all had cigarettes in their hands or in their mouths; even the lone staff member in the room, who sat at the counter, clicking away at his own laptop, had a cigarette set into the corner of his lips.

I walked up to the counter, holding my breath in my cheeks. As I got closer, I spied a whole range of gadgets behind the guy sitting there, mainly phones and cameras, along with bits of computer hardware and printer cartridges. A notice I could barely read in the room's dim lighting was stuck on to his checkout till, announcing the sale of discounted SIM cards and cartridge refills at rock-bottom prices.

"Hi," I called out to the man, exhaling. "Excuse me, is Michael here?"

"Huh?" He looked at me with a dazed expression. His shoulder-length hair was tied back in an unruly ponytail, and it swung about as he shook his head at me. "Bro, I told you already, you're gonna have to pay for something if you want to hang out here."

"Uh, I just got here. I'm Michael Lee's brother. Did you see him come in? Do you know him? Michael Lee Geck Soo?"

"I don't know, man! Hey, are you gonna pay up, or do I have to use the fire extinguisher on you again?"

"Right, okay, I'll just go up and play some pool then ..."

There was a landing and a flight of steps opposite the counter, and I headed there. "Hey! Hey!" he called out suddenly. "We don't allow dorks here!"

"What? I'm not a dork."

He started to get out of his seat. "Only cool people are allowed here, boy. You don't look like a cool guy to me; you look like a little dork," he explained. "A little dork who talks too much."

He advanced on me, forcing me to back up against the stairs. I peeked quickly at the two customers sitting by the computers; they remained lost in their fantasy worlds, oblivious to the scene developing right under their noses. I considered crying out to Mohidin for help, but decided against that option in the blink of an eye; with all that I'd been through so far, and survived, I was sure I could handle this guy by myself.

"Hey, man ... Bro, I'm cool," I said, flashing him what I hoped was a smile that exuded pure, unabashed confidence. "I didn't go to school today. I don't go most days. I hate class and homework and assemblies …"

He stood in front of me, glaring down. "Do you think I'm stupid, man? Just get the hell out."

It was make or break time, and I had to think of something fast. "I am super cool, bro. Trust me. I'll show you, okay?" I reached up and deftly plucked out the cigarette from his pale, grey lips.

"Hey, what the fu-ppppbt!" His tongue inadvertently followed the cigarette out, interrupting his curse with a splutter.

I had seen enough movies to know what to do, so I casually flipped the cigarette into my own mouth (trying not to think of the man's saliva that lined the outside of its brown filter) and took a quick drag, making sure not to ingest or inhale any of the smoke. I stored it all in my mouth, and then after a few seconds, when I couldn't bear to hold it in any longer, I blew it all out as smoothly as I could.

The counter guy was a little dumbstruck, and I took another puff. This second one did make me go a bit queasy, but I held it in long enough to convince him I did this often. I gave him another of my best grins before handing him back the cigarette.

"Whoa, you're like a pro, dude …"

"Hey, I smoke, like, a hundred of these a day. I'm cool."

"Y-yeah, man, yeah. You are cool. Go on up and enjoy."

The weirdo crawled back to his dingy counter, and I turned to the stairwell behind me. Perhaps that second puff had been a little too ambitious; I was struck by a bout of dizziness when I attempted to climb the staircase. I didn't know whether to curse that cigarette or to be thankful that it had helped me get past that monitor of all things cool. Why did smoking have to be the most popular pastime among these clowns? I would've preferred sniffing a hundred Kiko Cat glue bottles to smoking even a single cigarette.

When I arrived upstairs, I found that it was indeed the actual "pool" part of the pool centre. The place was an open hall with a layout that was bare to the bone: undecorated walls coated with flaking-over blue paint, a TV screening the afternoon news bulletin with the volume turned down, and a handful of worn-out pool tables stationed on a floor covered in plain, greyish-white tiles, each the size of a generic large postage stamp but with half the charisma – the kind of tiles I'd only seen before in school toilets.

I noticed that it was quieter here than the computer section downstairs. There were a few small groups of people gathered around the tables, but there were no sounds coming from them except for the frequent clacks of cue balls knocking together. The place felt so muted that I actually started to wonder if I'd gone deaf as a result of being exposed to all that smoke downstairs. One never knew when or where those *poklan* mutations might strike after all.

I noticed that there was another counter here, with another counter guy; thinner than the one downstairs and, amazingly, not smoking. Come to think of it, there was as little smoke on this floor as there was noise, and I didn't feel like coughing or puking anymore. Breathing comfortably, I stepped a little further into the hall. A clock near the TV showed that it was 1.59 p.m. Was I too late?

I ventured beyond the railings of the staircase, and walked on towards the tables so I could get a better look at this floor's customers. Most were facing away from me, but I noticed quickly enough that none of them seemed to be the same height as or have the same hairstyle as my lanky and shaggy-haired elder brother – Michael could be considered a giant by local standards. No, they were all short as well as short-haired, shooting their balls around lazily.

None of them seemed to have the energy or interest to notice me gawping and moving towards them. The counter guy was busy texting on his phone, and the patrons carried on like I didn't exist, allowing me to get in and amongst the tables and the players. On closer inspection, I realised that many of them were actually a lot older than your run-of-the-mill *poklan*. They were quite old, in fact; there were a couple of people here who even looked to be in their mid-30s or older, and were balding. But there was nobody who looked like my brother, or like any of his band mates, based on what I could recall of their faces from that picture I had seen on Kevin's phone.

No, keep calm, I stressed to myself in my head, trying not to lose hope. Maybe Michael wasn't here yet. Being around half an hour late was the usual for him, so I probably hadn't missed him. I hadn't even finished examining the faces of all these customers either; maybe one of them would turn out to be someone I'd recognise as Michael's friend. With a renewed drive, I moved in deeper, desperate to spot anyone remotely familiar.

And then I froze, terrified, for there he was. With his shaved head and flame tattoo on the back of his neck, standing by one of the tables. Baldie, from that gang of *poklans* who'd accosted me earlier. He should've been in a jail or a mental hospital by now. Had the school not been able to nab him and his crew before they could make their escape?

The guy had his back to me. Warily, I started moving about in a circle, aiming to steal a peek at his face to confirm my suspicions, yet trying not to reveal myself to him. As I approached him, I grew less certain that it was Baldie. This guy was probably a bit too short to be Baldie. His head just about edged past the level of the table ... Then again, he was probably simply bending down a little. I'd have to see his face to know for sure. Only a few more footsteps ...

A few more footsteps that had me walk directly into another customer's leg and cue, just as he was lining up a shot. He jumped away from me with a squeal of fright, knocking the wooden pole against the frame of the table in the process and alerting everyone in the hall, including Baldie, who straightened up ... and up and up until he stood at least a head taller than everyone else in the room. And then he turned around.

"Michael! You shaved your head!"

"Jonathan!" My now-bald brother was wearing the same horrified expression he had when I had accidentally broken his guitar once. "What the hell are you doing here?"

"Hey, man, move away. I'm trying to shoot." The man I had bumped into shooed me away, and I scrambled towards Michael.

"Wow, you look so different ..."

"I don't know why or how you got here, but you have to get out now!" Michael pointed emphatically in the direction of the staircase and then charged at me like an angry rhino.

"Michael, wait! Listen to me!" How does one stop a rhino?

"Go home, go to class, go wherever you want to, but just get the hell out of here. I can't be seen with you!" He grabbed at my sleeve and began dragging me towards the staircase.

With the only weapon I had at my disposal. "Hey, Michael, listen! *Ah Kong* died! He's dead and we're having the funeral!"

This stopped him in his tracks. For a few moments, anyway. "That's sick, Jonathan. That's just sick." He caught hold of my shirt and started to pull again.

"I'm not lying! Look at my clothes! Why would I be wearing funeral clothes otherwise, of all things? We tried calling ..."

Michael stopped once more, breathless. "Don't ... Don't mess around, Jonathan," he panted, tired from the effort of trying to haul me across the room.

"I'm not messing around! Why else would I come all the way from *Ah Peh*'s house to find you? I came to let you know and ... Are those earrings?" There was a silver stud in each of his earlobes. Also, an extra ring had been pushed into the upper part of his left ear. There were more changes to him of course – the flame tattoo on his neck wasn't the only one he had. Both his forearms were covered in greenish-black, swirling filigree patterns that seemed too random to mean anything.

"Don't make stuff up like this, Jonathan. It's not funny."

"I'm not making it up! If you called the house, they'd tell you the same."

"You're not serious ... Wh-when did he," he said with a slight gasp.

Finally, it was sinking in. "Yesterday. He had a bad chest. Nobody expected it."

"Why didn't you call me?" he shouted, nostrils flaring and eyes welling up.

"We did! You were the second person Pa tried calling, after Mum! You didn't answer. You haven't answered ever since you left."

"Fuck." Michael put a hand over his eyes. "Shit ... This is ..."

I'd never seen my elder brother cry before, and it was weird and deeply uncomfortable, to see it happen now; I'd obviously underestimated how much *Ah Kong* had meant to him. I knew from the movies I had watched that this was where I had to step in and give him a hug as a show of brotherly solidarity, but it was Michael we were talking about here, so I wasn't so inclined to hug him. Especially with all the snot and tears dribbling down his face.

"So ... Well ... There's something else ..."

"What?" He wiped his face then looked at me with bloodshot eyes. "Did someone else die?"

"No! It's about Mum. Have you been talking to her?"

"Huh? What do you mean?" He looked away.

"On the phone. Kevin said that you speak to her."

"That little shit! I told him not to say anything to you."

"So is it true? She's never coming back? Pa called her yesterday, and she said she was moving to Dubai and ..."

Michael gave me a look that was halfway between a smirk and a pitiful grimace. "They don't know crap ..." He sniffed. "Mum's not moving to Dubai."

"What? She's not?"

"She's not going to live there permanently. Maybe she is going there for a while but ..." He paused to blow his nose. I waited impatiently for him to continue. "Well, in any case, I don't think she's coming back home again. After helping out her friend there she'll just head back to Australia."

He rubbed his eyes with the back of his hand and straightened his stance. "That's why I'll be going to Australia too. As soon as I have the money."

"She's never coming back to Brunei?"

"No. Never."

The confirmation from Michael was a stab through my heart, a swift and sharp stab that went in so deep I felt it emptying my lungs of their air.

"Why isn't she coming back? It's been six months! I thought she got herself enough rest?" I gasped, suddenly finding it difficult to breathe.

Michael sighed. After a long pause, he simply said, "Australia is just where she's happy ... Where she's better off."

"Better off than being around us?" Ah, there was the knife again, just when I thought it couldn't twist itself in any harder and deeper.

"No ..." He gave me that pitying look once more. I wondered if I looked as miserable as I had in the mirror last night. Doubtless he'd find a time to poke fun at me for this later.

"Well, maybe she won't be gone forever ... I might be wrong. She didn't really say, alright? All she said was she didn't think she'd be coming back in a while."

That wasn't a very promising alternative, but it was better than "forever".

"Never mind anyway," I said, trying to sound brave. I didn't want to talk or even think about the chances of my mother's prolonged absence anymore. "I came here mainly to call her. So I can speak to her before she leaves for Dubai."

"You want me to call her? Now?"

"Yes, now! If she might never be coming back home, then that's only more reason for me to talk to her, isn't it? Besides, I haven't spoken to her in months!"

My brother stood there, unsure about what to say or do.

"Get her on your phone, Michael!" I insisted with such

determination that I surprised both myself and Michael. He quickly pulled out the phone from his pocket.

"But if I do this, then you gotta take me back to the funeral. Deal?" he said, fingers hovering over the touch screen.

"Huh? You want to come along?"

"Of course I do, you idiot! It's *Ah Kong* we're talking about, not our pet dog or something."

"Don't blame me for asking. It's not like you ever gave me the impression you cared that much about the family ... But why do you need me to take you? What happened to your motorbike?"

"I don't own one yet, okay. And I'm not old enough for a licence anyway."

"Since when did something like that stop you?"

"Feeling a little cocky, you little wiseass? There's a lot you don't know about me so shut your mouth ... How did you get here anyway?"

"Well, long story short, I'm not with anyone from the family. I escaped the funeral and hitched a ride here."

"What the f ... I don't believe it. Who gave you the ride?"

"I'll tell you later, okay? Just get Mum on the phone now before she gets on the plane!"

"Alright, sheesh!" He began tapping some numbers into the phone. "I don't know, she may have already left the house by now ..."

"Hurry up then!"

"Okay, it's dialling! It's ..." He stopped, phone to his ear and a frown on his face. I stood in position, my hand coiled back in preparation so I could snatch the phone away from him the minute my mother answered.

"Ah, shit. I ran out of credit."

"What? How could you?" I felt myself shivering with anger. How could he have been so careless? So dim-witted? My expectations of him had been nothing but rock bottom, and yet he'd failed to even come close to meeting them.

"You idiot!" I grabbed his shirt and yanked at it as I yelled up at him. "I can't talk to her because you forgot to watch your balance? Go and top it up now!"

"Frickin' hell, Jonathan! Stop wrecking my shirt!" He tried to swat me away, but I didn't let go. "I was going to do it after this, so sue me."

"After what?"

"After this. The pool game. How do you think I've been making money?" He swept an exasperated arm across the pool tables and the players. "I'm not here for fun. If you'd just let me finish one game …"

"You don't have any money now? It's five dollars minimum!" I loosened my grip on him, then let go completely.

"That's five dollars more than what I have! You've been hanging around with Kevin too much huh? You think money springs out of everything?"

"Well, what about the internet? You can reach her on 3G, can't you?"

"You need credit for that too, genius."

"Then …" I had to think of something. Damn it, I was too close to just give up now. "I know, we can use Kevin's phone. He's on a contract. Just give me the number …" And then I remembered that my cousin's phone was out of power.

"I need a charger. Do they have any downstairs?"

"I don't know. Maybe …"

"We'll just borrow it. Come." When Michael hesitated, I

grabbed him and then pulled him along as I rushed down the flight of stairs. I went up to the ponytailed oaf behind the counter and produced Kevin's phone. There was no sign of Mohidin in the hall yet, but I was all too aware of the fact that time was running out for me, both in terms of getting hold of Mum and in delaying his entry into the pool centre.

"Hey, uh, do you have a charger for this one?" I asked the man. "I need to use it to call my mother. To pick me up."

"Huh? Yeah, I think so ..." He absentmindedly fished out a brand new one, still packed in its rigid plastic box. "Twenty dollars."

"Um. I meant, could we borrow one?"

"What? Borrow? This ain't a charity, dude."

"I know ... But it's an emergency! My brother's sick and ..."

The guy flashed Michael a skeptical look. "He doesn't look so sick to me, bro."

"Please? See the ... See his hair? It's all gone because of the chemo he's had. He needs to talk to our mother who ... who'll pick us up from here, because he isn't feeling too good now."

"Jonathan! What the hell are you doing?"Michael growled under his breath, but I ignored him. I kept my eyes fixed on the guy at the counter, who was looking back and forth between me and my bald brother, trying to make up his mind.

"Ah, okay," he said at last. I had to stop myself from pumping my fist in the air. He pulled out a white charger, presumably his own personal one, and plugged it into one of the nearby sockets before heading back to his computer. I immediately attached Kevin's phone to the connector, and put it on the counter before us.

"I'll never forgive you for this, you stinking turd," Michael whispered to me through gritted teeth.

"I didn't see you coming up with a better idea, you moron," I hissed back.

As I watched, a power indicator flashed up on the phone's otherwise blank, black screen a few moments after I had attached it to the charger. And a few moments after that, I pressed and held on to the on-button, and the whole thing came back to life.

But back to a screen that asked for a four-digit password. A password that only Kevin knew.

"Oh, damn it!" I cried aloud. "I thought he'd taken the password down!"

"Must have been just the key lock," Michael scoffed. "Not the opening password."

"But … how do I do this now?"

"Don't ask me. Call Kevin yourself if you want."

No. I had a better idea.

"We can switch SIM cards. Kevin's should work on your phone."

Michael proceeded to fiddle with his phone while I did the same with Kevin's. I'd never handled a smartphone before today, so finding out where the SIM went was new to me. If only it was as straightforward as a regular one …

"Ah, let me do it," Michael grunted, relieving me of the phone. "You wouldn't know where to find it if it bit you in the ass." He got the SIM out with ease and did the switcheroo for me as well. Then, when the phone powered up, he brought up the digital number pad and began dialling Mum's number.

"Here you go." He handed over the phone to me. "Now you can finally get off my back."

I collected it greedily with two hands, shuddering with

anticipation as I listened to the dial tone beep away. Now, at long last, after all the near-misses, all the stumbling blocks, and all the drama I had been through, I was finally going to get what I wanted. The phone was slick with sweat from my temple as well my palms as I adjusted and re-adjusted it against my right ear. The tone was still ringing steadily, so no cause for alarm yet.

"Hey, does she usually take this long to answer?" I checked with Michael.

"Have some patience, toadstool. Wait a bit."

Oh, I could wait alright. I'd only been waiting six months for the chance to speak to her ...

The dial tone stopped, and so did my heart momentarily.

"*The number you have dialled is not available at this time. Please try again later ...*"

No! Horrified, I let go of the phone. It fell to the floor, and was saved only by a hair's breadth by Michael, who managed to catch it before it crashed down. He went on to cuss at me in the most profane way he could manage, but none of that mattered to me.

I wanted to puke. All that I'd suffered through the day ... It had been for this? It was all over now. I had come so far for nothing. I closed my eyes and let the oncoming surge of crushing despair wash over me. Deep down, maybe I'd known all along that this was always going to be the most likely result of my quest. That I was going to fail. When I opened my eyes again, I saw Michael standing there, nursing his phone like a newborn baby and staring grimly at me.

"Anything else you want me to do?" he mocked.

"Yeah, there is," I said. "You can come home with me now. Let's get out of here. We've got to get back to the funeral."

Chapter Thirteen

Mohidin was waiting for us outside. I was relieved to find him there, but my brother stiffened and grew rather uncomfortable at the sight of him.

"Hi, Mohidin. We're done," I called out, raising a tired hand in greeting. "Here, this is my brother, Michael ..."

My new friend ignored me. "You!" He pointed an accusatory finger at my brother. "So, you've been hiding in here this whole time."

"Uh, yeah, I ..." Michael stood rooted to his spot, and was suddenly sweating profusely.

"What's going on? You know him already, Mohidin?"

"Yes, very well. He and his friends have visited my shop before. And they've taken a lot of things from me without paying."

"Michael! How could you!"

"I ... It was just ... Come on!"

"You owe me two boxes of cigarettes! That's two hundred dollars, and now I know who you are. Give me back my money, or I'll call the police," Mohidin threatened, wagging his finger at my brother.

"Hey, Mohidin, please listen to me," Michael said in a trembling voice. "I'm going to my grandfather's funeral today and ... and when I get there, my father will give me the money to pay you back. Yeah, take me and my brother home and you'll get your money." Michael nodded his head and grinned squeamishly at his accuser.

"Yes, could you take us back, please?" I joined in. "My father will pay for him. I can guarantee it," I pleaded, and I hoped I sounded convincing, because I had my doubts about whether Pa would really do that for Michael.

"Ah ... I don't know about that ..." Mohidin shook his head at me.

"Please, Mohidin? Trust me. We'll get your money back. And I'll make him swear he'll never steal again." I glared at my brother.

"I swear I won't steal again," Michael mumbled.

I tried again. "Please? I promise, on my life."

Mohidin gave my brother a doubting stare then turned to me. "Oh, okay ..." he conceded grudgingly. "He's lucky you're his brother."

"Yes, he is." I glanced knowingly across to Michael, who did his best to not respond with an obscene gesture in front of his creditor. "Don't you have something to say to Mohidin?"

"Well ... I ..."

"Forget it," Mohidin rejected the stuttered beginnings of Michael's insincere apology. "Let's go, boy," he said to me, and then left abruptly, leaving the two of us to trail behind him.

"Hey!" Michael hissed at me when he was just out of our earshot. "You're supposed to defend me, toadstool! Why the hell are you even friends with this guy anyway?"

"Because he really helped me out, okay. And why should I defend you? You're a bloody thief!" I shot back. "And frankly, I'm surprised you haven't been put in jail yet."

"Shut up, toad!" He gave me a whack to the back of my head, and I retaliated by elbowing him in the knee.

"Ow! You little … I'll get you for this."

"You just try!"

Mohidin jerked his head around to glare at us, and we both settled down; Michael even put an arm around my shoulder as if I were suddenly his best friend. He followed that up with a not-so friendly noogie when Mohidin looked away.

"Hey, by the way, how did you know where to find me anyhow?" Michael asked, shoving me out of his grip.

"Ow … You're 'friends' with Kevin online so we just looked through your pictures," I replied, rubbing my sore crown. "One of them had some messages about you coming here today to meet someone."

We left the block and walked back out onto the street. The afternoon glare that came off the burnished surfaces of the cars and the road signs burned blazing imprints into my eyes, and both Michael and I paused to raise our hands up to shield out the sun.

"Isn't your friend going to miss you?"

"Ah, screw him. He forgot, as usual."

"Are you playing pool for money? What happened to becoming a rock star and all that crap?"

"When I get to Australia, I'll finally have the space to do what I want to do. Till then, I'm laying low."

"You sure are doing a good job at that," I rolled my eyes at him.

"Hey, when I become a famous rock star, you'll all be begging to be known as my siblings. And I'll have a whale of a time seeing you all suck up to me … Scramble around to get favours from me. Especially you."

"Fat chance. The only thing you'll be fit to do over there is to farm kangaroos." Michael took a swipe at me, but I ducked and dashed ahead, crossing to the other side of the street and then running back to the department store where Mohidin had parked the car. Michael followed suit, and we soon found ourselves sitting in the car, getting out of Badir.

Surprisingly, the traffic was now a lot lighter than what I was anticipating, and we managed to return to the highway rather quickly. From the front passenger seat, I gave to Mohidin a series of general directions that would take us back to *Ah Peh*'s house. It was unfortunate that my faithful friend had returned to his phlegmatic demeanour and blank expressions from when I first met him in the shop; if anything, he was even less conversant now than before, probably owing to my brother's presence in the backseat.

Mercifully, Michael seemed to be wallowing in his own thoughts, and wasn't doing or saying anything that might have offended our driver. The glove compartment was closed, and I was glad that he couldn't see what was inside; he could see the big round object in the plastic bag next to him though, but his response to it had been to keep himself as far away from it as possible, and to avoid looking at it (though I did notice him giving it the occasional curious eyeball).

Within minutes, the highway took us past the international airport, providing us with good views of the runway, the matchstick-shaped control tower and part of the terminal. Immediately adjacent to the airport grounds was a small golf course; I had always considered this an odd choice of venue for a game that was supposed to rely on relaxation and concentration. On the other side of the road was soft, flattened earth with a rudimentary running track that was earmarked for further development into a recreational park (again, this close to planes taking off?). Further in the distance was the national stadium, its four towering floodlights standing out against the horizon. Partially blocking our view of the airport was a small hill. The whole side of it facing the road had been cleaved away, and was covered in concrete and shaped into three gigantic steps resembling the start of an enormous staircase. My father had explained that this served to stop any landslides from happening and from damaging the road. Seeing this hill always gave me this urge to climb it with ice-picks and ropes like a mountaineer, for then I could climb down the other side and find out if the same thing had been done to it as well. I always tried to catch a glimpse of this hidden face of the hill every time I went past it, but I'd not yet been successful.

It was strange; my quest had ended in abject failure, yet here I was, feeling a strange kind of calm. Why I was feeling so composed after the soul-destroying outcome of my outing was still anyone's guess. But by now, I was too tired to care. I'd done what I could, and there weren't any choices I could say I truly wished I hadn't made.

"Mikhail," Mohidin uttered, all of a sudden and unprompted.

"What?" I perked up in my seat.

"My brother's name was Mikhail. It's Arabic for Michael. What a coincidence, huh?"

"I guess ..." From the corner of my eye I saw my Michael trying to look like he wasn't paying attention to us. "Was he ..."

"He was about twenty when I was your age. I remember my grandfather buying him a motorbike for his birthday. His first one, just after he got his license. Took me for a ride to celebrate."

"We crashed into one of the parked cars at the first junction, probably less than five hundred metres from our house." Mohidin's voice did not waver, nor did his face change when he said this. "He always wanted to go full speed in everything he did, and so it was with the bike too. When I woke up, I was in hospital again, and stayed there for almost a month. Hurt my head badly apparently. I still need medication for it.

"Mikhail died on the spot of course. Someone must have been protecting me, but not him. So it's good that you're looking out for your brother."

He stopped and continued driving silently. In all honesty, there was nothing I could think of saying in answer to his tale, so I nodded understandingly, hoping he'd been able to sense my token of condolences, even if he didn't acknowledge it. Michael sniffed and turned his nose up and away from us.

Mohidin didn't speak much after that, and neither did I. Eventually, the car came to a halt just outside the grounds of *Ah Peh*'s house. Mohidin saw the crowd gathered outside the house and took in all the funeral paraphernalia, but looked more interested in it than put off. Unlike Michael, who had his gaze fixed firmly at the floor of the car.

"Bet you've never been to a Chinese funeral, have you?" I asked Mohidin.

"No ... I don't think you've ever been to a Malay one, either," he replied.

"No, I haven't," I admitted. "Actually, this is my first funeral ever. Of any kind."

"I'll let you know the next time there's one you can attend ..."

"Thanks, Mohidin ... Thanks for trusting me. Anyone else would have refused to help."

I started to take my borrowed sandals off. "I guess I should give these back now."

"Keep them. It's alright."

"Are you sure? I can ..."

"No, I'm sure. Don't worry, you deserve them. And not once did I ever think that you were lying to me, boy. Tok Dodol can always tell when someone is."

Or so he thought.

"Okay, thanks again," I said sheepishly. "By the way, you can call me Jonathan."

"Jonathan."

"I promise we'll repay the money Michael owes you." As I said this, I heard my brother open the car door and rush out, leaving me behind.

"Hey!" Mohidin shouted after him. "Hey! Running won't help you. I'll remember you!"

"Don't worry," I intervened. "I'll get my father to come over and talk to you now."

Mohidin shook his head. "No, it's not the right time. Not now."

"But ... Okay then, we'll return the money once this is over. What's your phone number? I'll give you a ring when I've got it."

He wrote it into a scrap of paper and gave it to me. Likewise, I provided him with the number for my house's landline.

"Now, I should go," Mohidin said. "And you should too ... Your family's waiting for you."

I took one last sweeping look at the car's interior before stepping out. This was my final chance to ask my friend about the thing in the plastic bag, still sitting roundly on the backseat. Well, maybe another time. Mohidin threw a quick wave and drove off, leaving me staring after the car. I waited until it had disappeared completely out of view.

And then it was back to business.

A number of changes had been made to the house while I had been away. Banners with Chinese inscriptions had been hung everywhere, and a large tent made of red and yellow canopy, and supported by a number of sturdy metal poles now occupied a substantial portion of the area in front of the house's main doorway. In the middle of the tent was a casket, placed upon a platform covered in a white cloth, probably the same one that *Ah Kong*'s body had been laid on earlier in the day. The altar had also been shifted to outside the yellow-red tent; it still carried the black-and-white portrait of *Ah Kong*, as well as the urn, which now held three thicker-than-usual joss sticks that had burnt down almost to their stumps. Near the tent, many rows of red plastic chairs had been set up, presumably for seating the guests for tomorrow's ceremony.

Kevin's father was standing amongst these chairs now, talking to a couple of guests whom I didn't recognise. Frida and Kevin were at the front porch, squatting over the basin containing the circle of fire. Aaron was nowhere to be seen, and neither was Pa, which made both Michael and me ease up considerably.

My Plan A was based on the assumption that no-one had figured out yet that I'd left the house, in which case I'd simply have to show Michael around and amp-up the "happy surprise" element of his unexpected homecoming. If they'd sussed it out that I'd escaped, then Plan B would be set in motion, and I would try and justify Michael's return as something worth going AWOL for.

We approached *Ah Peh* slowly, me walking several footsteps ahead of my elder brother, who was shuffling along so reluctantly that I had to eventually drag him along by the hand.

"Shit, man … I don't think I can do this," he murmured.

"You big baby … Come on!" I made it clear that Michael was winning no sympathy from me. If he couldn't be brave out here, then how could he act so inside, in front of Pa?

Our little exchange did serve to attract the attention of our uncle, who dropped his conversation with the guests and rushed over. He waved his arms in the air madly as he jogged towards us, and his cries were just as frantic. "Michael! You're here!"

"Hi, *Ah Peh* …" Michael greeted him, gulping down hard.

Ah Peh stopped in front of us, out of breath and staring dumbly at our faces. Frida and Kevin noticed us as well and they stared too, but they stayed where they were.

"I-I-I've … I'll get your father," our uncle finally stammered, bursting off and then stopping halfway and shuffling back to us as if he had changed his mind. "No, wait, you'd better come inside! Follow me. You have to change, Michael. And meet your father. Come in."

Ah Peh yanked Michael from his spot and into the house, brusquely brushing past his own children who were perched near the main door. And that was that. It looked like I had got away with it after all.

I walked over to my cousins to see what they were up to.

"Hi guys … Did you see that? Looks like nobody found out," I said with a relieved smile.

Kevin glanced towards the front door. "So you brought him back? Did you get to speak to your Mum?"

"Wait, you went out?" Frida blurted. "You left the house?"

"No, I didn't. I think I was too late," I sighed, ignoring Frida. "Did my father say anything? Did anyone suspect I was gone?"

"I don't know. I pretty much stayed out of his way since you left," continued Kevin. "Jonathan, I don't think you know but …"

"Hellloooo, can someone answer me?" Frida interrupted us again. "Did you actually escape, Jonathan? So you've been gone all this while?"

"Yeah, I did leave the house, Frida. And what don't I know, Kevin?"

"How did you leave?" She just wouldn't let it go.

"Um … Around lunch time earlier," Kevin began hesitantly, "your mother … She called the house."

I waited for the calmness inside me to die a sudden death, to be scorched away by an explosive outburst of pent-up anguish. I winced in preparation and … Nothing happened. I simply took this in; it was just another missed call, another missed opportunity. I could stand it. At least I had tried, hadn't I? And I didn't think I'd ever get too distraught by anything else as terrible I'd ever experience in life, not with today's events as the benchmark.

It suddenly came to me that after six months of my mother's absence, and after doing nothing but simply sitting on a forlorn hope to see her and talk to her, this had been my first attempt at doing something about it. Even though I didn't get to speak to her, and although I knew that anything I might have tried to persuade her to come back home would never have worked anyway, I still felt quite content with the outcome of my adventure. I'd brought Michael home after all. If nothing else, that was something both Mum and *Ah Kong* would have been happy to see.

"Nobody's allowed to leave once the ceremony starts with the wake. You broke the rules, Jonathan …" Frida continued, but I wasn't listening. I walked on, towards the front door of the house. I noticed some activity going on inside; did I dare go in to see how

Michael's reunion with my father was faring? The image in my head was a cringeworthy one, and yet I couldn't help but want to see for myself, so through the door I went.

Where the altar and the platform had been placed before, there was only empty space now. And in the middle of that space stood Michael and my father. *Ah Koh* was by the door to the hallway, ignoring the few guests who were still inside the house, and observing intently the confrontation between my father and brother, which must have been a great replacement for all the Japanese soap operas she was missing that day on account of the ceremony. *Ah Peh* and *Ah Em* floated around Pa and Michael, half-coaxing them and half-twittering to each other about how amazing it was that my brother had come back just in time for *Ah Kong*'s funeral.

An anticipatory tension filled the room; everyone was waiting for either Pa or Michael to make the first move. I knew it was going to take a while though. Pa had his arms folded tightly in front of him, and had his face tilted back so he could face his much taller son. This was his no-surrender pose, and not once in their very rocky history had he ever been the one to relent. Pa gave permission and granted things; he didn't ask for favours nor did he make offers. My elder brother, on the other hand, was looking down at his feet glumly, and fidgeting away with his hands in his pockets; he didn't look like he was going to speak anytime soon either.

Ah Peh and *Ah Em* eventually gave up and hushed themselves to a complete silence, and joined the rest of us in an exercise of mental nail-biting. The only sign of movement from Pa was his heavy raspy breathing as his chest rose and fell beneath his rigidly folded forearms. It seemed like he hadn't even blinked from the moment I entered.

"I ... I came back, Pa," Michael mumbled, still looking at the ground. Everyone breathed a sigh of relief, save for my father, who continued with his hard, unyielding stare.

"I ... I'm sorry. *Ah Kong* ..." Michael's voice broke, and he shifted around as if an insect had crawled up his trouser leg.

Oh, Michael, please don't break down now. Not in front of all these people.

"Michael." Pa finally said through gritted teeth. "How did you know to come about your *Ah Kong*?"

"Jonathan. He ... He messaged me, and I saw it late last night. I'm sorry I didn't answer the phone."

The oppressive, uneasy climate that had descended upon the room only thickened now. Pa tensed and leaned backwards even more, then took in a sharp breath of air. I decided to step in and do something quickly to diffuse the situation, but I was beaten to it by Pa himself, for he sighed and shook his head, finally relaxing his arms and letting them go limp by his side.

"Go upstairs and get changed," he said to Michael, and then turned to me. "Jonathan, go and find some funeral clothes for him."

I nodded and started moving across the room. As I passed my father, he leaned in towards me and whispered ominously, "You stay upstairs. I want to talk to you." Then, he motioned for Michael and me to hurry on up. A very familiar shadow of impending doom hovered over me as I headed upstairs.

My brother and I spent the next five minutes ransacking Kevin's room in the hope of finding something that would fit Michael as well as my father's requirements for proper funeral clothes. We settled on a pair of navy blue tracksuit bottoms, but on Michael, they came off more like a pair of three-quarter shorts. Deeming that as acceptable enough, we moved on to the shirt, which turned out to be much more difficult to obtain in his size. Although I knew full well that I would be in a great amount of trouble if I were to get caught, I excused myself and went to *Ah Kong*'s room to rummage some more. There, I managed to fish out an old tobacco-stained blue shirt from the cupboard we'd missed last night. I gave it to Michael, but lied that it was from *Ah Peh*'s room. The funeral ensemble piled up in his hands, my brother left the room and headed to the bathroom to get dressed.

A few minutes after he had left, Pa arrived in the room to have his little chat with me, storming in as he often did and shutting the door firmly behind him. Just the two of us then, with no-one else to witness the massacre.

"Jonathan, where were you the whole day?" he drew his question out slowly, each word heavy and deliberate.

"What do you mean, Pa? I was around ..." Now it was my turn to shift and fidget while staring at the floor.

"Look at me!" he snapped, and I flinched before automatically looking up to face my father. "Where have you been all day?"

"I was helping out here ..."

"Don't lie to me!" he interrupted. "Your brother was trying to cover for you, but I know you left the house."

I had nothing to say in return.

"Now, I want to hear it from you. The whole truth."

There was no hiding it from him anymore. Why even try?

"Yes, Pa, I did."

To my surprise, the infuriated screaming I expected from him did not materialise. Pa was keeping steady. And I could see that his face was softening slowly.

"It was for your Mum, wasn't it?"

"Yes."

"Do you know that she called earlier today?"

"Yes."

"Did you manage to speak to her over there?"

I shook my head. I bit into my lip to keep myself under control. This control over what I could feel … I couldn't let it slip away. I wasn't going to let my father of all people see me break down.

"Well, then," he looked away and sighed, giving me just enough time to compose myself. "There's nothing more to do, is there?" He then turned back to me and moved closer, hitching down so that his own face was almost to the level of mine.

"But this is the only time you'll ever do something like this, understand?" he said with a finger stuck out and pointed at the tip of my nose. "That was dangerous, and stupid. And if you hide things like that from people …" He broke off and got up, his eyes, as ever, staring authoritatively down his nose at me.

"I won't do it again," I said.

He nodded curtly, and then he gave me a look he had never given me before. The look definitely wasn't friendly, but neither was it hostile. It was like … like the look he usually had on his face whenever he conversed with other adults.

"I am sorry, and I won't do it again, Pa," I repeated. "I messed it up for myself. But, at least Michael's back."

He grunted. "Yes, and *Ah Kong* would have wanted that …" He walked past me to open the door for himself. "Oh, one more thing, Jonathan." He halted with one foot out of the room. "Your mother asked for you. You really disappointed her by not being here when she called."

I didn't know what to feel – jubilation for finally being asked for by my mother, or sullying guilt for having let her down. Maybe both, and much more too, all at the same time.

"I asked her if she could call again, for you …" he continued. "And she said she will. Once she's reached Dubai, probably tomorrow evening. Our time." With that, Pa swiftly left the room and headed back downstairs, leaving me dumbstruck by the reversal of my fortune. And to have such good fortune come to me from him of all people … Could I afford myself a smile? Should I go ahead and give myself a hi-five to celebrate?

No, it would be best to wait to do that, until I was actually speaking to her. I didn't want to jinx it already.

Michael peeked around the door just then. "Is he gone?"

"Yeah."

"Shoot," he said, emerging out of his hidey hole. "I heard all that."

"Okay …"

"It's funny that Mum called the house, huh?" he slapped my back and guffawed. "All that work, when you could've just stayed here and spoken to her. You should've spent more time thinking about it."

"You'd better not go there," I warned him. "If not for me, you wouldn't be here so you owe me big time." That served to shut him right up. "And you should talk. Why don't you spend your time thinking of something useful, huh?" I continued. "Like thinking of an excuse to give Pa about the cigarettes you stole and the money you need to pay back to Mohidin."

While my brother stared at me uneasily and struggled to come up with a retort, I made my exit, walking out of the room and back to the funeral.

Chapter Fourteen

The events of the day had left me worn out, but there were plenty of chores to do, and I wasn't spared from having to pitch in.

I headed over to the porch where Michael and Kevin were seated, tending to the circle of fire. They were unsupervised, which was a rather unwise move on the adults' part. In spite of this, the circular trail of ever-burning paper was still going strong, the mound of ash upon which it sat heaping up dangerously close to the brim of the container.

"What's this supposed to mean?" I asked as I joined them. "Is it supposed to be sending up money to *Ah Kong*?"

"It's the circle of life, idiot," Michael answered, scoffing. "Don't you know anything?"

"We're lighting up the way to heaven for *Ah Kong*," Kevin explained more patiently. "We need to keep doing this until the burial."

"What if it goes out?"

"We can't let that happen."

"But what if it does? Will *Ah Kong* get trapped in limbo? And then he won't get to heaven?"

"That's crap, man. That doesn't make sense." Michael leaned forwards to feed another couple of pieces into the burning trail. "You kids are so dumb."

"See if I burn anything for your funeral ..." Kevin mumbled.

"Hey, man, when I die, I want none of this shit done for me. Just put me in a hole with my axe, and I'll rest happily for eternity."

"This is tradition," I tried to argue. "We're showing our respect to *Ah Kong*."

My brother rolled his eyes at me, and then glared at Kevin. "And fat boy, don't be so sure about being around for my funeral. I don't think your heart can keep supporting all that weight for much longer."

"Oh, yeah?" Kevin was disconcerted, but tried to maintain an air of nonchalance. "Well, you're probably going to catch AIDS in jail before I drop dead."

"That's it!" Michael bolted upright, his legs kicking out and almost upsetting the circle of fire. "I am done here!"

Kevin reared back with fear in anticipation of a beating, but my brother simply turned tail and walked away, probably to help himself to some smokes.

The two of us kept the burning going in relative silence. I got the sense that Kevin was finally in an appropriate mood for the occasion, more solemn compared to this morning or yesterday. He wasn't even curious to know about my excursion, although I was itching to fill him in on all the dramatic details of my adventure.

Over at the tent, *Ah Em* and *Ah Koh* were busy making miniature ingots out of red and yellow paper, with blessings written on them for burning at the burial tomorrow, while also maintaining the vigil over *Ah Kong*. Jen was by their side, folding away under the direction of her aunts

"Where're the others?" I asked Kevin.

"Inside. I think Frida and Aaron are resting."

I could've done with a nap myself, but felt obliged to soldier on without rest or refreshment, largely out of guilt that I had bailed on the morning's duties. After an hour of watching the fire with Kevin, I swapped places with my sister. I picked up the ingot-making with ease, quickly managing to outpace my aunts, who were busy chattering away about their yoga classes and gossiping about our various guests from the morning. Their conversation nearly sent me off to sleep; nothing genuinely interesting seemed to have occurred in the house that day, from what I could gather

When Aaron came back out to help us, he was the chirpy, upbeat Aaron I had known all my life. Evidently, he'd had a good chat with Mum and whatever she'd told him must have lifted his spirits. Trust Michael to try and make it seem like the world was ending; I was going to take only Mum's word for what she had planned for the future. All I had to do now was wait until after the funeral for that long-awaited phone call with her.

By the time dinner was ready, the adults had gained enough trust in Aaron and me to leave the two of us alone with *Ah Kong*'s body while they grabbed a quick bite to eat. Kevin also went in, leaving a refreshed Frida (who was usually on a diet anyway) to take over his job of guarding the circle of fire.

Of course, the first thing my younger brother wanted to know, for it was now safe for us to talk, was all about my grand day out. I began narrating my tale to him, including my horrific encounters with the dogs and the *poklans*.

"Wow, you met real *poklans*? Could you speak their language? What were they like?"

"Nuts." That was the most succinct way I could put it across to him. "They drive around in stupid cars all day, looking for glue to smell and schools to spray-paint."

"Wow, that's so dangerous!"

"I never want to see another *poklan* again as long as I live."

Aaron mm-hmm'd in agreement, but didn't seem too convinced that the *poklans* were indeed truly terrible.

"So … was Mum about to leave when she called?" I asked before I could move on to the next part of my tale. "You know I left to call her, but I couldn't get through …"

"Yes, she was probably in the airport already then. Hey, Kevin's coming out!"

My brother pointed to our cousin, who was emerging from the front door, a plate of food in hand. He looked a bit shaken, and gloomier than before, as he stumbled to the edge of the porch and flopped down to take his meal. I watched as my cousin sat there, not eating, and I knew something was wrong. Frida carried on with her duty and acted as though nothing was amiss, but I sensed that she could tell something was up with Kevin too. The sight of him poking and picking at his food rather than finishing it all in quick mouthfuls was a sight I never thought I'd live to see.

"Look at that! He's not eating! For once in his life, food is actually second to something else!" Aaron squealed, pulling an exaggerated look of bewilderment. "I don't believe it …"

Neither could I. "Hey, stay with *Ah Kong*, Aaron," I said. "I'll go see what's wrong with Kevin."

I expected Kevin to be evasive or uncooperative, but speaking to him turned out to be an utterly useless pursuit. All he said was that the adults were not speaking at all, neither amongst themselves nor to him, and that there was a very uncomfortable silence in the dining room, which had forced him to seek a better spot to have his dinner. On my pressing further, Frida answered for him instead and asked that I drop the matter. Naturally, the adults were being awkward, she said, because they were still dealing with *Ah Kong*'s death, and Kevin was merely being a big, fussy baby about not getting any attention from them. I went back to join Aaron under the tent.

"What did you find out?"

"Nothing. The adults aren't talking, and Kevin wasn't getting enough attention, so he left ..." My brother could see I wasn't convinced by this reason. "Hey, Aaron, you were with him the whole day. What's wrong with him? Did something happen?"

"Why? What's wrong with Kevin?"

"I'm asking you!" I said, growing exasperated. "Well? You were here!"

"I don't know ... We were just doing our chores ... Normal stuff." Aaron paused for a moment, as if he had just thought of something. "Well, he did disappear when the Malacca Lady came over."

It wasn't surprising that she'd dropped by to proffer some form of spiritual advice for the funeral, and I for one was glad that I'd missed meeting her. I'd seen her in action before, during a blessing ceremony organised by *Ah Em* for this very house, and she had behaved even bossier than Mrs. Yap on the day. She'd gone around the house like a woman possessed, ranting and raving at the adults, ordering them to move that chair there, lest a ghost sit in it, or to move a picture here, lest a ghost come out of it, or to reinstall the lights on another side of the room, because that would keep the ghosts from hiding in that corner. Kevin had been absolutely terrified of her then, and her presence today must have stoked those fears afresh.

"Did she do anything? Cast a spell on him or something?"

"No, I don't think she even met Kevin. I think I only saw her talking to *Ah Em* ... Nothing unusual, really."

Just then, *Ah Em*, *Ah Peh* and my father stepped out of the house, letting Frida, Aaron and me to take our turn for dinner. We were having yesterday's leftovers, reheated and refried, but I wasn't complaining; this was my first proper meal of the day, and I was too hungry to care about taste and freshness.

After dinner, we resumed our duties. Unlike yesterday, there would be no bunking-off upstairs to play around; we were to maintain the vigil through the night, and even Aaron wouldn't be spared. It wasn't an arduous task by any stretch of imagination though; we were scheduled to go to bed at 1.00 a.m., and Aaron and I had slept later than that time on a number of occasions. However, there was one small problem – I was to spend most of the night with Uncle Ben, and that wasn't something I looked forward to doing. He and I were to handle watching over *Ah Kong* in the tent, while Aaron and Michael were in charge of burning the paper at the circle of fire.

The setting sun was met with the emergence of a swarm of small bats, smaller than the ones I'd disturbed back at the abandoned house, chittering animatedly as they began their hunt for bugs. The smoke from the circle of fire and the joss sticks at the altar kept most of the insects and especially the mosquitoes away from us, but I did see occasional flying forms swooping down to attack the house's drains.

The ever-darkening orange hue of the evening sky soon gave way to a deep indigo. A chorus of high-pitched croaks commenced around us, the hungry cries of the garden frogs, who were also coming out to have their dinner. I thought of Pak Tut, nestled away in his cage at the back. Did he dream of the freedom to hunt all the creatures flying and roaming around Kevin's garden? Did he even want to do that anymore? How much ambition could there be left in the lizard who got his meals minced up and hand-delivered, twice a day and with seasonings?

Uncle Ben sauntered over to me and sat down on the chair beside me. He gave me the sort of look that one would give a puppy born with no limbs, or to a beggar-child with no eyes. I gave him the same look back.

"So, Jonathan ... How are you feeling?"

"I'm okay."

"Oh, your poor, poor *Ah Kong* ... Why do the good die so young?"

"He was 78 ..."

"I mean, he was such a wonderful man, your grandfather." Uncle Ben's voice cracked. "Kind and generous and loving. You know what he said to me on my wedding day? He said that, for once, here was a man who deserved to be the one to take his daughter off his hands ... Shelter her, pay her bills, indulge her every whim ... He loved me like I was one of his own! I'll never be able to repay him."

"Right ..."

"I feel like a hug ... Come on, Jonathan, give Ol' Ben a hug."

Cringing to myself, yet unable to come up with an excuse to get out of it, I got off my seat and placed a light hand on his right shoulder, holding my breath the instant I got a whiff of the overpowering mothball smell coming off him. He lifted himself off his chair to embrace me all the way.

"Hey, let's get the other two over here," he said when he let go of me. "We'll have a nice get-together. There's no rule about having to burn the paper so far away from the tent, is there?"

"I don't know. You're the one in charge."

"Well, it can't hurt, can it?" he clucked. "Hey! Hey, Michael!

Aaron! No need to stay so far away! Come on over here!"

Aaron and Michael looked at each other with obviously reluctant expressions, but after a bit of annoyed eyebrow twitching and nostril flaring, they came over to join us, bringing their evening's work with them.

"What's the problem, Uncle Ben?" Michael asked.

"No problem. Just thought a little chat would be good for everyone."

I almost snorted at that.

"Why don't we share some stories, huh? I was telling Jonathan about the time I got married to your *Ah Koh*. We were at the part right after I proposed and took her to see my parents."

"But I thought she forced you to marry her," blurted Aaron. I flashed him a warning glare, but he missed it completely.

"Ah, ha ha," Uncle Ben laughed nervously. "What? Where did you hear that?"

"*Ah Koh* told us. She said that you kept staying over at her place, and that everyone was talking, so she had to keep scolding you until …"

"Oooooh, your *Ah Koh* was just pulling your leg, boy! What a sense of humour, huh?" Uncle Ben laughed again, but his face had turned a bit red. "Anyway, your *Ah Kong* … What a man he was. Taking in a guy like me, with not much money or status, and still giving me all his trust."

"Wow, that was great of him," Aaron piped in.

"Indeed it was, Aaron."

"Yes, even though you have abnormal testicles."

I couldn't help but burst into a fit of giggles, but then forced myself to look serious again. Michael covered his mouth and laughed into his hand. Uncle Ben looked mortified.

"Wh-what? How did you know? I mean ..."

"Oh, I thought *everybody* knew," Aaron said, seemingly confused about what was so funny about what he had said.

"Right, er ... You know, that's not ..." Uncle Ben came to a stuttering stop then looked desperately between the three of us and the coffin in which our grandfather was resting. "Ah, I need to go to the toilet. Sorry." Uncle Ben promptly sprang off his seat and ran back into the security of Kevin's house. Once he was inside, Michael and I broke into the loud bursts of laughter we'd been suppressing for the past few minutes.

"I can't believe you told him that!" I chortled. "Where's your common sense? Now he's gone running to *Ah Koh* to tell on us. She'll be here any second to pinch us into saying sorry."

"Oh no! Her pinches hurt!" Aaron wailed.

"Well, at least he's gone. Finally!" Michael declared. "Can't believe I have to spend the whole friggin' night with that clown ..."

Minutes later, once the laughter had died away, I began to worry in earnest about how awkward it would be if or when Uncle Ben came back from the house. It had all come out in front of our dead grandfather, and in hindsight, it felt like we'd crossed a line along the way. But considering the type of man he'd been in life, I doubted that *Ah Kong* would have cared too much. In fact, there had been times when he had sided with us kids when one of the adults made complaints about our wild and unruly behaviour. At least, up until that fateful day he chanced upon us setting off fireworks next to the gas cylinders in Kevin's kitchen.

"Now what? That was kind of rude. It won't be very comfortable when he comes back, with or without *Ah Koh*."

"Whatever, man. All I know is that I'm happy he's not here

…" Michael whipped out a cigarette and lit it with the fire from the burning papers. "And I can have a little of this without any worry."

"Hey, isn't that disrespectful to *Ah Kong*?"

"I'm lighting up to his memory, shitface. Have you never heard of toasting to the dead? Actually, since he used to smoke, it's probably disrespectful that you two aren't lighting up."

"Why don't you let me try?" Aaron tried his luck.

"Fuck off. Go buy your own."

"You don't want to smoke, Aaron," I warned him. "Look at what you could turn into," I pointed to our elder brother.

Michael presented me with a vulgar hand gesture.

"Way to prove my point, Michael. Seriously, how long do you think Uncle Ben's going to take? He can't leave us three alone here."

"I don't care …"

He took a drag, leaving Aaron to take charge of keeping *Ah Kong*'s trail to heaven going. The ingot-making activity entrusted to me had been left untouched for a fair while.

"I can't believe that idiot might get a share of the inheritance," Michael snorted. "And to think *Ah Kong* was such a tight-ass …"

"That's probably where Pa gets it from."

"Pa? Don't even compare him to *Ah Kong*! Our grandfather was like … Axl Rose and Bono combined compared to Pa. Our father's just a miserable bastard who can't enjoy anything in life and has to shit all over us to let it out."

"Hey, Pa's not that bad!" I argued.

"You're practically his clone, that's why you're defending him. *Ah Kong* was twice the man that Pa could ever be. Hell, he lived through the Japanese Occupation and almost got killed by those soldiers ..."

"Almost killed by soldiers? I've never heard that story."

"Is it the one with the stomach ache?" Aaron butted in.

"He knows." Michael smirked at me.

"How the hell ... How come I don't know about this?"

"That's 'cause you're such a loser."

"Shut up." I turned to my little brother. "Aaron, what happened with *Ah Kong* and the soldiers?"

"Pa told me that when *Ah Kong* was a boy, he had to help out at his father's shop by making small deliveries. One day, he happened to have a bad stomach ache, but he was forced to run to one of the other shops to deliver a bundle of cigarettes. A group of Japanese soldiers bumped into him along the way and stopped him. He was so scared that he forgot to salute and just stood there. The soldiers got angry, and the angrier they got, the more scared *Ah Kong* became and the worse his stomach ache got. Finally, it became too much for him, so he ran to the roadside, took down his pants and went 'ppprrraaappp' right in front of them."

Aaron brought his hands to his buttocks then waved them downwards for illustration. Michael wrinkled his nose at this.

"What did the soldiers do?"

"They laughed and then rushed off pinching their noses."

"Wow, I really didn't know about that one," I chuckled.

"There're loads more that you don't know. I bet you can't think of a better story about *Ah Kong*, can you?" Michael challenged.

"Well, I do know one. Remember *Ah Kong*'s Goddess of Mercy idol? The one you tried to grab off that high shelf because you thought it was topless? Oh, all the pieces I could count when it crashed to the floor. "

"How do you ..." Michael was open-mouthed in amazement. "That must've been ... Were you even born then?"

"Of course I was! You just think everyone else has a lousy memory like yours," I tutted. "Does your ass still smart from the whacking he gave you for that?"

"Shut up, toadstool!" He flicked his cigarette straight at me, and it landed on my left arm with a burning sting. Yowling in pain, I jumped off the ground, and in doing so, accidentally kicked at the basin containing the circle of fire, spilling black ash all over Aaron's trousers. He, in turn, jumped back as well, causing the burning paper folds to spill out and extinguish completely.

"You dickhead! Look what you did!" I screamed at Michael.

"You're the clumsy idiot! Don't blame me!"

"Oh no, it's everywhere!" Aaron frantically dusted himself down.

"What did you throw that cigarette at me for? This is your fault!"

"Jeez, it was only a cigarette butt. Who asked you to act like such a girl, toadstool?"

"Who asked you to act like such a moron, gecko? Now we're all screwed."

"Guys, we'd better get this back together. Otherwise *Ah Kong* will never get to heaven!"

"This is just a bowl of dust, okay? And there's no such thing as heaven, Aaron. How old are you?"

"He's eight, Michael. Still acts older than you do though."

"Want to get burned again, toadstool?" Michael waved a fresh cigarette at me.

Ignoring him, I set the tipped-over basin back to its rightful position and retrieved the scattered paper folds. Almost all of the ash was dumped on the ground around us, and wasn't worth attempting to scoop up. However, fearing that their presence might attract unwanted attention tomorrow, I pressed my shoes into the piles of ash and worked them into the ground.

"What are you doing with your foot? Nobody's going to notice or care," muttered Michael, a newly-lit cigarette sitting between his lips, and his legs crossed ever so casually

"You could help me out here, you know," I grumbled.

"Fine." He picked up one of the folds and ignited it with his smokestick. He then placed it in the basin, and Aaron picked up from where he left off, building a new chain of fire that sat deep within the ash-depleted container.

"Hurry up! Uncle Ben's coming back!" I urged my younger brother, after noticing the front door opening slowly.

We resumed our original positions by the time Uncle Ben had returned to his seat. He acted as if the entire dialogue about his testicles had never happened, and that worked just fine for us. He didn't notice the spilled ash either. Instead, he continued recounting the memories of his courting of our aunt and trying to make *Ah Kong* seem like a Bruneian version of the Dalai Lama. Personally, I'd have preferred hearing more interesting stories about my grandfather's life and adventures during the Japanese Occupation and the rebellion of the '60s. Or even anything to do with how *Ah Kong* had dealt with my parents' marriage.

My parents had met in Manchester, where they'd both been sent on government scholarships. Given the opportunity to experience the carefree, independent lives of university students in England, only my mother had seized the chance to make the most of her time there; what I'd gathered from the snatches of conversations I'd overheard between the adults was that Mum had accumulated a wealth of experience partying and travelling, as well as getting into a string of relationships with numerous men, by the time she had hooked up with my father. What my parents had seen in each other back then, nobody knew; they probably didn't know themselves.

Inevitably, Mum's reputation set the stage for the confrontations ahead. Both *Ah Kong* and *Ah Ma* had considered her a no-good floozy who'd squander their son's inheritance and their legacy, and they'd shared this belief with Pa, poisoning his mind against Mum from the beginning. Even after things became a little more cordial between Mum and her in-laws, she had probably never gained their full blessing. As far as I'd heard, Pa would always take his parents' side in any dispute between his parents and Mum, especially about her going out in the evenings without him or getting involved in activities that he (and they) didn't approve of. After all, everyone knew the heartbreaking story about her dance class.

Mum had been a very talented ballroom dancer during her undergraduate days in England, and a frequent prize-winner in a number of inter-university competitions. Sadly, there was little hope of continuing her interest once she returned home, but the spark never died down, and she was desperate to keep dancing. A few years later, after doing some research, she had managed to devise a business plan for setting up a small dance class she hoped to run on a part time basis with a friend.

The idea never came through, however, because of opposition from my father's side of the family. They argued that a good wife should spend all her evenings supervising her children and tending to her husband, and that it'd be improper for her to show her body off to, and get into close physical contact with, strangers outside the family, especially strangers who were men. Because Mum would have been the main source of capital (via her late father's savings), as well as the main instructor, her friend was unable to go ahead without her, and the whole project had collapsed. It was almost twenty years since she last danced, but even up to the days before her leaving for Australia, I could remember her reminiscing about the tours she had been on and her performing in fancy ballrooms.

I was brought back to the present and to our vigil over *Ah Kong*'s body by the sound of Uncles Ben's loud and melodramatic sighs. I realised that he had probably said something extremely emotional, and wanted us to react to it. His droning continued, and he narrated one boring story after another, but we tried our best to tune him out. He eventually nodded off at a quarter past midnight, his head lolling back against his chair and snoring lightly with his mouth wide open.

"Hey, let's put something inside it!"

"Don't, Michael. You're in enough trouble already!"

"You're such a killjoy, you know? Jeez, you're as bad as Jen."

"No, I'm not!"

"Oh, yes, you are," Michael sneered, then stretched out his hands and yawned. "I am so bored. I was waiting for this idiot to fall asleep so I could take a little break."

"A break? Now?"

"Yeah, now. My hands are fucking killing me." And with that, he got up and left.

"Where's he going?" Aaron wondered.

We saw him walk past the front entrance and disappear behind a corner.

"I don't care. Probably for a smoke."

"Well, now that he's gone, can you please finish your story? I want to know more about Mohidin."

I wasn't in the mood, but if I didn't do it now, Aaron would keep pestering me about it until I blew a fuse or a major blood vessel, so I gave an almighty sigh before continuing with the narration of my adventures in Badir. I was quite thorough and even included the details of my conversations with Mohidin, but excluded anything that indicated or hinted at his weirder side; I did tell Aaron about Michael stealing from Mohidin and about the money he owed him. My younger brother lapped up everything I said then fired a barrage of questions about every single aspect of every single point I'd mentioned.

"And what about that Mohidin? What a nice man he is, huh?"

"Yeah, nice guy ..."

"I can't believe Michael would steal from him. We've got to get his money back somehow." And then he went on to ask me more questions.

I answered them all until I was out of reserves, and then all I wanted to do was hit the sack. My little brother continued to show an eagerness to interrogate me further, but he soon got the idea that I was done for the day.

"It's almost time. I'm sleepy," I said.

"Yeah."

"I hope Michael isn't sleeping in our room tonight."

"No, he's sleeping in the living room upstairs. He's got the whole room to himself."

"Why don't the adults use the upstairs? I don't know why they want to sleep on the floor ..."

"Maybe they want to be closer to *Ah Kong*?"

"Yeah, that makes sense … Hey, what's Michael up to? He's been gone for a while now. Aaron, go sneak up on him. Any trouble from him will cause trouble for all of us."

Ever the eager beaver, Aaron sprinted off towards the house, in the same direction that our elder brother had headed off in. I sat back, waiting for him to return with some news, hoping Michael wasn't up to anything worse than smoking.

Aaron returned barely moments after he'd rounded the corner.

"He's just sitting there by himself."

"Ah, leave him then."

"But, you know, he was talking so much tonight," Aaron said gleefully. "He never used to talk so much to us."

"Yeah, but now the problem is getting him to stop …"

I suddenly heard the sound of footsteps coming our way, and saw a figure approaching us. It turned out to be *Ah Peh*, ready to start his shift early.

"Ah, hi, *Ah Peh*," I greeted. He didn't respond to me, focusing instead on his sleeping brother-in-law.

"Ben! Wake up!" he said in an annoyed voice. Uncle Ben gurgled and rolled his head about a little but didn't wake up. *Ah Peh* went up to him and gave his arm a rough tug. That did the trick, but surprised Uncle Ben so much so that he jolted awake, his arms flailing wildly, and fell off the chair and to the ground, tipping over a bag of ingots.

Aaron burst out laughing, and that got him a very stern look from *Ah Peh*. Our uncle ordered us back into the house but neglected to ask us about where Michael had gone, distracted as he was by Uncle Ben's antics. We went inside, bypassing the other adults asleep in the downstairs living room on our way upstairs and into Kevin's room. Sleep hadn't seemed this inviting to me in a long, long while.

After some speedy teeth-brushing, I confidently expected that I'd fall asleep the moment my head hit the pillow. Yet again, for some reason, I couldn't. And the more the minutes ticked on, the more frustrated I got, knowing and feeling how tired I was but still unable to find a way to fall into a few hours of restful shut-eye.

I listened to Aaron's quiet and even breathing and assumed that he'd found slumber without any problems. Kevin's respirations, too, sounded restful; he'd remained undisturbed all the way through our entry into his room and our bedtime preparations ...

"Jonathan?"

But asleep he wasn't.

"Yeah, Kevin? You haven't slept yet?"

"No, I can't. Hey, do you still have my phone?"

"Yes, it's here. Still in my pocket." I fumbled around for the phone under the blanket. When I found it, I reached up to hand it to my cousin. "Here you go. But, oh wait, the SIM card is still with Michael ..."

"Never mind, we can change it tomorrow." He got quiet after that, but I could hear his breathing come out in quick, sighing bursts.

"Are you okay, Kevin?" I knew the answer to my own question; my cousin didn't seem okay at all.

"No," he said after a few moments. "The Malacca Lady was here today. She told me I had a ... a ghost on my back."

"A what?" I had to keep myself from laughing. Kevin sounded serious.

"A ghost. It's following me around and bringing me bad luck. She can see it!"

"That doesn't make sense," I said to him while lying in a comfortable supine position and with my eyes closed. Maybe all this nattering was the cure for my insomnia.

"I thought maybe it could be *Ah Kong*, upset about Michael not being here ..."

"In that case you're safe, aren't you? He won't hurt you."

"But what if it's not him? What if it's something that stayed behind after I used the magic board? How do I get rid of it?"

"You used it during the funeral? I thought you said it was dangerous to do that. You even asked Aaron not to use it."

"It was just before the funeral actually. I only wanted to know if *Ah Kong* was alright ..."

"So did you get anything? Did you get to speak to *Ah Kong*? Or anyone else?"

"Not really ..."

"Then there's probably nothing to worry about."

"But she said she can see it on my back! And the only way for me to get rid of it is to wear this *hu* for 40 days. She said it will protect me."

"Then wear it. It's just a piece of red plastic."

"But will it work? What if it doesn't? And the ghost stays with me forever?"

Now he was getting plain irritating. I wanted to end this as quickly as I could. "You believed her about the ghost, so you might as well believe her about that charm thingy."

An imaginary solution to an imaginary problem – how ideal.

"Are you sure?"

"Yes, I'm sure. Now, go to sleep."

"But I'm still scared ..."

I gave him a loud groan to show how annoyed I was getting

of this. "Just pray to *Ah Kong*. If you can believe all that crap that lady told you, then you might as well believe that he'll protect you. Now, stop keeping me awake."

Kevin stopped talking, and for a moment I thought I was finally going to get the quiet I needed to fall asleep. But then he called out for me again.

"Yes?" I replied.

"Do you miss *Ah Kong*?"

"I guess, yeah. I do."

"You don't look it."

Why did Kevin say it like that? Was he trying to make me feel guilty?

"I don't know, Kevin ... I guess I didn't know him well enough to feel truly sad about it. I didn't see him often. And I don't think he knew me too well either." It was true that I didn't know *Ah Kong* that well, and I was definitely never doted on by him, like Kevin had been, nor had I lived with him for the better part of the last decade.

"He liked you a lot, Jonathan. Maybe he never said it to you, but sometimes, when I was alone with him, he'd tell me to study more so I could become as smart as you."

"Right! As smart as me," I replied skeptically. "Hah. Maybe my father was reading out make-believe exam results to him all this time."

"No, he really meant it ..." Kevin trailed off, and I thought that this was the end of the conversation. Finally. Now, I could try to get some sleep ...

"I'm sorry, Jonathan," he blurted out once more. "About yesterday. About getting you into trouble. I did it because ... I'm jealous of you."

"Jealous? Of me?"

"I don't know why ... The more I thought about what *Ah Kong* said about you, the more I wanted to act that way. And wanted to make you mad."

I should've given him an earful over that confession, but considering that he had apologised to me and had actually confessed to being jealous of me, I decided to give it a pass.

"Forget it. It doesn't matter anymore. You were the one who was closer to *Ah Kong*. Nothing can take that away," I offered. "You know ... for me, maybe I'd have felt differently if he and I had spoken more. So, yeah, I guess I wish I'd known him better. That would've been kind of nice in a way ..."

My cousin got all quiet again, and I assumed it was another attempt to lull me into a false sense of security before he could bug me with more annoying questions. But he didn't do that this time around. He had nodded off for real, leaving me to wonder as to how much of that unintentional ramble he'd actually heard. Well, it wasn't going to be repeated tomorrow or ever again for his benefit, should he manage to remember this conversation and the awkward sentiment he'd somehow got me to express openly, against my better instincts.

Chapter Fifteen

I was standing outside the house, keeping watch over the coffin all on my own, the world around me pitch black and as still as death itself. The front door opened, and someone came out to join me.

I turned to look, and saw that it was a boy. A boy about my height and my size, walking over to where I was standing, and I recognised him the instant he was close enough. The boy was me.

It felt so strange to see this, yet, I wasn't afraid. And as soon as he had reached me, pictures of that boy's life began floating through my head, flitting glimpses of the things that I'd been told about him. I saw the boy on a ship leaving China, waving goodbye to his parents for that would be the last time he'd ever see them. I saw him toiling away at a sewing machine from dawn till dusk in the backroom of his foster family's shop, the skin of his fingers raw and blistered. I saw him getting reprimanded by his foster father for not being subservient enough. Getting reprimanded by customers for not being subservient enough. Getting reprimanded by soldiers for not being subservient enough. I saw him taking it all, patiently, not speaking a word in return. I saw him growing up, getting married, buying his own shop, then two more shops, then four more ...

When the boy reached my side, the images faded. There we were, the two of us standing in front of the coffin, neither speaking to the other, but both knowing exactly what we had to do. A basin containing a ready-made, self-perpetuating circle of fire was at our feet, and we began throwing things inside it, for them to burn. I started with a ripe banana, and my companion threw in something wrapped up in brown sackcloth with roots dangling out of it. Then I tossed in a chewed-up sandal, and he the obituary page from today's newspaper. Then, he turned to look at me. And he disappeared, right before my eyes.

And where he had stood only a moment ago lay a doll now, lifeless and inanimate. I picked it up and held it in my hands, bringing its eyes in line with mine. The boy had transformed into this marionette, and it still had my face, and it was staring right at me.

It was obvious what I had to do next.

Looking down at the basin before me, I held out the doll then dropped it into the fire. Folding my arms, I stood back to watch it burn, feeling quite right with myself and with the world as that face continued to look up at me, almost imploringly, while its sides singed and turned black, and yet the face itself somehow resisted complete incineration by the flames that had enveloped it.

Why wasn't he burning properly? I reached out a hand to test the fire myself.

And that was when the alarm clock woke me.

Why had we set it so early again? Ah, yes. Today was the day we were going to bury my grandfather.

By the time I had got downstairs, everyone else was already seated at the kitchen table for breakfast, except for *Ah Em* and *Ah Koh*, who were outside carrying out the wake. We all looked tired and worn out to varying degrees, the girls coming off the worst with their puffy eyes and drained faces. Even Frida didn't look as perfect as she usually did, and was caught half-dozing off in between bites of her sandwich. Mugs of hot tea went untouched, and little was said between the adults. Even Uncle Ben looked serious, though that might have had something to do with getting busted by *Ah Peh* for sleeping on the job, and the earful he must have received for it.

A little relief seemed to come our way, however, when some close relatives and family friends started arriving to give their last respects to *Ah Kong* before the burial. A touch of joviality even returned to both *Ah Peh* and Uncle Ben's demeanour, and they started to smile again as they spread themselves out amongst the guests.

This time, there were no serving duties allotted to us children for the few hours until the ceremony began. Crates of fruit juice packs were stacked up near the seated area for the guests to help themselves to, and that was about it in terms of the day's refreshments.

Of course, I soon discovered that this didn't necessarily mean we were free to do as we pleased. Aaron and I were ushered back to the ingots and the circle of fire to relieve the ladies, and Michael was similarly exiled to sitting through this duty with us.

"This is even worse than yesterday …"

"No kidding, Michael."

"This is all so screwed up. I can't believe I let you talk me into coming here."

"You wanted to come here, remember?" I snapped back. "Look, everyone's tired. It'll be better once it's all over."

"Yeah, right …"

The three of us toiled away in silence, without any energy left in us to talk or fight. Free to let my mind wander, I allowed it to drift back to thoughts of yesterday's events – the creepy house, the crazy *poklans*, my strange friend Mohidin – all the while carrying on with the paper folding with the least amount of diligence I could muster. I carried on in this trance-like state until Pa walked up to us to announce that the ceremony was about to begin.

We watched on as a middle-aged man dressed in a green polo shirt and cargo shorts picked up a microphone and began making announcements in Mandarin. We couldn't understand him, not only because we didn't know any Mandarin, but also because the speaker to which he was hooked was broadcasting a sound so fuzzy it sounded like he was talking through a mouth stuffed with a swarm of cicadas. Fortunately, a second person was available to translate the instructions for the non-Mandarin speakers present, of whom there were a fair few, including many of the deceased's own kin.

We were told to stop with the ingot-making and the circle of fire, so Aaron, Michael and I left behind our duties to join our father near the altar. I peeked back at the untended bags and basin, and felt a little guilty about deserting them. The fire must have gone out by now, I realised with some unease, and wondered if *Ah Kong* had made it to his final destination on time.

The girls and *Ah Em* emerged from the house and stood beside us. Only one person from the family was missing now. Well, two persons actually, if you counted Mum, but I wasn't sure if anyone was really keeping count of her.

"Pa, where's *Ah Ma*?" I asked.

"She's inside."

"Why?"

"The wife isn't supposed to join in, Jonathan. Only the children and grandchildren do," *Ah Em*, who was standing next to me, explained.

"Yeah, but she's the wife. Isn't she the person who needs to say goodbye the most?"

"Oh, such a sweet boy," *Ah Em* cooed. "No, it's tradition. *Ah Ma* has to stay there for the rest of the funeral, and she can't follow us to the grave. But she's okay. Her family is in the house with her."

I still felt sorry for my grandmother. But before I could challenge her absence again, the MC's distorted voice boomed through the speaker and announced that it was 10.00, thus time for us to commence the ceremony. Apparently, it was up to us bereaved descendants to start things off, and as with traditional Chinese hierarchy, it was to begin with *Ah Peh*, who was *Ah Kong*'s eldest son.

The MC removed himself from the microphone and walked over to hand my uncle the framed black-and-white photograph of *Ah Kong* from the altar. Clutching it with both hands, *Ah Peh* got down on his knees and proceeded to drag himself through the grass and soil around the coffin. The sight of my big, important uncle doing this in front of us and the guests caught me off guard, and I stared in shocked silence as he completed three such rounds with absolute compliance.

When *Ah Peh* was finished, my father was given a bamboo staff, thin and flimsy but nearly two metres long and with a white flag tied to its tip. He propped it onto one shoulder, the flag-end dangling high above him, and repeated my uncle's actions just as devotedly and subserviently, making for a viewing that was just as unsettling to watch. Down on his knees and bent forwards, his head bowed low, he crawled around *Ah Kong* three times, his face as hard and clenched as it usually was. I was sure that the image would stay with me long after the funeral was over; this man whom I would've never thought capable of bowing down to anyone under any circumstance was doing it here so willingly. When he was finished, it was *Ah Koh*'s turn, who executed the coffin-crawl holding on to a paper umbrella.

Ah Em and Uncle Ben as the in-laws followed suit, empty-handed, and then it was down to us grandchildren. We were given no items to hold on to either, but we were provided an additional instruction to get on with it on both our hands and knees. The funeral customs mandated this as a mark of respect, the MC informed us.

While going around the casket on all fours, I realised to my horror that the ground was much damper than it looked. Muddy soil squeezed in through the gaps between my fingers and caked on to my fingernails each time I planted a palm down. The worst part was when I accidentally touched a patch of stripped-off earth on the other side of the coffin, closer to the guests, while finishing my first circle. Pasty, greyish-brown muck got stuck all over my hands, making me balk with disgust as I recalled that this was the exact same patch that two stray dogs had messed up a year ago, and the neighbour's mutt the year before that.

The ickiness notwithstanding, I trampled on as fast as my limbs would take me, and completed the circles without showing my hesitation to my family or our guests, and only noting to avoid the bare spot on the next two passes. When I was done, I rejoined my relatives and saw out Aaron as he finished off his last circle around our grandfather.

Then came the prayers, and this was to go family by family, again according to hierarchy. The portrait was returned to its original position on the altar, and we knelt down before it to pray with joss sticks, and then got up before kneeling down once again for another round. We did three such rounds in total, and when we were done, the MC handed us a bottle of liquor and instructed that we empty a bit of its contents onto the ground.

I noticed a bit of a stir amongst the onlookers when *Ah Peh* and Kevin did this together, and very generously with regard to the amount they offered their lawn. There was no such controversy with my father though, who tipped out only a little and without any request for assistance from his children.

When *Ah Koh* and Uncle Ben stepped away after their turn, it was time for the guests to pay their last respects. Watching on from afar, we observed them walking up to the altar in batches, each group making their prayers with joss sticks provided by *Ah Peh* and then planting them into the urn beside the portrait before making way for the next set of mourners.

Not far from this, a number of funeral workers were grouped around a black hearse that was resting on the driveway, its rear facing the tent, parked around the same place the coffin-truck had been yesterday. They looked to be biding their time until their services would be needed, doing little to fit in with the sea of sombre faces moving around them. Closer to the main gate was a second vehicle; a white minibus that I guessed would be our transport to the cemetery for the burial. Both the hearse and the bus had white funerary banners slung over them, probably as a sort of signal to help us have a smooth and unobstructed journey on the road.

Ah Koh walked over and squatted beside me.

"Do you know who all those people are?"

"Not really," I said, my eyes fixed on the proceedings of the ceremony.

"Let's see ... That group's from the Kinmen Association ...

Ah, and those two are people from the Lai family, of the Lai shipping company. See how they're all paying their respects to your *Ah Kong*? Look at that one; that man's the second son of the elder Lai, the patriarch of the Lais. Did you know that he owns about half of all the houses and shops in this area, on his own? Now imagine if I told you that he's the poorest son in his family! Amazing, yeah? If only I could find clients like that ..."

"Is it going to be over soon?" I wasn't terribly interested in where this conversation was heading, and I interrupted her so we could get back to talking about the proceedings.

"Yes, soon. Look, see those people over there? Those are my colleagues from the bank. Now, that's my boss. Do you know what a regional manager is? It's a very, very important person ..." She began to explain the intricacies of her job to me, and I didn't half understand her jargon-filled blabbering, nor did I really want to. She must have realised this, because she eventually gave up and went back to giving me a running commentary on the guests who had turned up for *Ah Kong*'s funeral, with particular attention to all their individual assets and holdings. I couldn't help but feel quite amazed that my aunt knew so much personal information about so many people, especially since she wasn't on close terms with most of them.

In all honesty, it was a bit surprising to conceive my grandfather having so many well-wishers and friends. Sure, he'd done his bit for charities and other philanthropic stuff, but I couldn't think of anything he'd done that deserved so much attention or affection, something truly extraordinary like saving a drowning man or winning a special prize from the Sultan. By all indications, he'd lived an ordinary life, and had been an ordinary person with a bit of good and a bit of bad (maybe more bad than good), like every other adult I knew.

Wave after wave of visitors kept streaming in towards the urn, filling it with a big mass of smoking incense that soon started to resemble a giant cigarette butt, and then flowed from the altar to the seated area. Like yesterday, it was cloudy this morning as well, but there was no sign of imminent rainfall fortunately, and we were probably going to get away with not having hired a second tent for the guests to shelter under. What we weren't going to get away with, however, was not providing enough chairs for the guests, and a number of them were forced to remain standing while others resorted to sharing seats. I could see why no-one was keen on planting their bums on Kevin's lawn, given what I'd gone through earlier.

After the last group of mourners had finished their prayers and moved along, the MC gave *Ah Peh* and Pa the go-ahead for the final part of the ceremony. All of us, being *Ah Kong*'s immediate family, gathered around the coffin and then gradually dispersed to the sides as the hearse reversed towards it, giving way for the funeral workers to get to the coffin. The MC called something out, and *Ah Peh* translated it for us, asking us all to turn away from *Ah Kong*, which we did in unison.

The MC then made another slightly longer announcement, and this time it was *Ah Em* who assumed the role of translator. "Okay, children," she said with a breaking voice. "When the man gives us the cue, you must all cry, okay? Don't turn around and look at the coffin but cry as loud as you can for *Ah Kong*."

She was cut off by the MC's signal, and immediately let out an impassioned wail, and was joined a split second later by the rest of us in a co-ordinated display of grief. Even Pa gave it his all, and this shocked me even more than the crawl he had done around the coffin. Amongst us grandchildren, Kevin, Frida and Jen seemed to be crying in earnest and sounded the most grief-stricken. Michael looked emotional, but wasn't quite on the same scale as them, although he was a lot more vocal than I'd have expected from him. Aaron was screaming out *Ah Kong*'s name, over and above everyone else, and I suspected that he was simply trying to be the loudest in the group.

I raised my own voice with the others, but I doubted that it lent a great deal more to the overall din being conveyed to our guests as well as to *Ah Ma* and her relatives indoors, and of course to *Ah Kong* himself, wherever he was at the moment. He'd lived through war, poverty, and above all, the trauma of having to bring up, and then put up with, this family for years; hopefully he was going to finally get the rest he very well deserved.

I also spared a thought for my grandmother, and wondered yet again if she would rather have been out here with all of us than stay confined to the inside of the house. Well, considering her stroke and all, I didn't know for sure how aware she might have been of the ceremony's proceedings and how much she'd have appreciated being allowed to watch us take her husband to his final resting place. Nonetheless, it didn't feel entirely appropriate that she wasn't outside here with the rest of the family.

At the MC's beckoning, we stopped with our cries and wails, and turned around to see that the coffin was now sitting inside the hearse. The vehicle was already facing away from the house's compound and was ready to go, and so were we.

As they entered the hearse, Pa, *Ah Peh* and *Ah Koh* were handed again the objects with which they'd paraded around the coffin. The car's confined interior was just enough to accommodate them, but it was so cramped in there that Pa's bamboo staff almost curled back in on itself, the flag on the other end nearly touching the floor between my father and *Ah Koh*. The in-laws and we grandchildren walked past the hearse and got into the minibus near the gate; it seated about twelve, including its front row. I found a seat at the back, and Kevin plopped himself down next to me.

"Oh, how come you're taking that?" I asked, pointing to his lap. He was carrying the basin full of ash from the now-extinguished circle of fire.

"Mum asked me to bring it along. See, they're bringing the ingots as well." He pointed to the bus's door, where a funeral worker leaned in to throw the bags onto the front seat. *Ah Em* was sitting closest to the bags, and was thus responsible for repositioning them so they didn't spill over on the way. All in all, we had five big sacks, which I thought made a good number for our efforts.

Once the hearse got started and moved past us, the workers closed the door to the bus, and our driver released the brakes, trailing behind the coffin and its bearers. The hearse glided along at a moderate pace, and our bus did the same, keeping to this speed even when we got on the main road. We didn't really need to step on the accelerator anyway, for we reached the outskirts of the cemetery in less than twenty minutes. I'd never been to this (or any other) cemetery before, but I did recognise the junction leading in to it. It was one that I'd passed by several times, and I remembered it most for its two parallel roads that went off in two different directions, one up a slope winding around the hill against which the main road ran, and the other that ran flat and eventually supplied a cluster of nearby houses and a power substation.

Though they weren't that far from the main road, these houses somehow managed to feel rather secluded to me, and more so than those ruins I'd encountered near the coffin warehouse. There were no cars, clothes on laundry lines, or any other signs of human habitation to be seen anywhere in the area, let alone people, and the houses themselves were no better, with their crumbling paint, moulding façades, and their lawns' grass grown to a height that wouldn't have looked out of place in the African savannah.

Untroubled by this road's meagre traffic, our convoy turned in, only for our minibus to take the lane that would lead to the houses while the hearse took the one that went uphill, into the cemetery proper. Evidently, I was the only one who was confused by this; everyone else seemed to be alright with the detour we were seemingly taking.

We parked at the compound of the first house, and I noticed that like all the others around it, this house was as empty as a *poklan*'s brain. After the minibus came to a stop, I got out and approached the abandoned shell of a home. Decay and neglect aside, it had probably made for a cosy little bungalow in its heyday, in spite of the distasteful coat of lemon-yellow paint it was covered in. I imagined a family living there, children and their parents playing and talking behind the house's closed, tinted windows, or walking about on its now dusty porch.

Standing on a clearing in the grass, only a few metres from the minibus, was a severely rusted-over canopy swing, listing badly from having partially sunk into the soft, pliable earth. It was a bit hard to tell if it had ever been used, or if it could still be used, and I started moving towards it with the aim of examining it a bit more thoroughly. It couldn't hurt to maybe give it a go now …

"Jonathan! What are you doing? We're going up!" I heard

Jen shout from behind me.

I turned around to see that the others had walked over to the beginning of the slope and were already some distance away from the minibus and its driver, who was sprawled across the front seats and settling into a nice late morning nap. Jen, peeved as ever, was gesturing wildly at me to hurry on up.

"Sorry," I shouted back as I raced to my family.

The procession was led by Kevin, who had the container of ash pressed to his chest. Michael and Uncle Ben followed close behind, carrying the bags of ingots, and *Ah Em*, Jen and Frida were next in line. Aaron and I trailed them, taking the opportunity to linger a bit and savour our surroundings, enthralled just by the thought that we were going to enter a cemetery for the first time in our lives.

It was a short walk to the top, where the ground levelled off into a plateau-like flattened area. The road stopped abruptly here, and we continued along a footpath that ended at the cemetery's gateway, a concrete structure painted in pink with a small, green-tiled roof at the top. Hanging below the roof's rafters was a wooden sign with Chinese characters inscribed on to it in gold against its black background, and below it, instead of a door, was a bar set across the gateway like a barrier at a tollbooth; it was currently lifted out of the way to let us walk in. The whole thing was set in the middle of a brick wall, also painted in pink. The hearse was parked alongside this wall, on ground that was more dust than soil and overrun by masses of weeds with spidery, finger-like tendrils. Camouflaged amongst this overgrowth was a nasty surprise that, fortunately, was presented to the leader of the pack and not the runt.

"Ewww!" Kevin cried, jumping to his right. "Dog poo! I just

stepped on it."

"Never mind, Kevin, just walk past it now," his mother urged him on.

"Arrgh! There's another one there!" He skipped to his left this time, dancing around the unsanitary obstacles.

Could those dogs not leave me in peace? I immediately stood on my tiptoes and trained my eyes to the ground, avidly hunting for any fresh brown forms as well as older whitish bits. Luckily, I did spot the deposits that my cousin had already alerted us about, and had contaminated himself with, and avoided them carefully as I joined the others in going through the gateway.

Once inside, the sight of all the gravestones spread over the cemetery's ground got me instantly interested. I had only seen them in books and movies before, where they were all Christian-style crosses. The ones here were very different, mostly mounds of grass-covered earth, each almost completely encircled by a waist-high ring of tiled-over concrete and with a large headstone at the front that displayed the deceased's picture and the dates of birth and death. Only a few of the graves were simpler, just beds filled in with pebbles or even plain concrete slabs accompanied by their markers.

Each one of these graves occupied quite a bit of space, leaving very little in the way of walking room between any two plots. Even the main path through the cemetery, which we were taking now, was narrowed down considerably by this congestion of graves, and its bottlenecked state was made much worse by an obvious utter lack of planning; many of the graves hadn't been set down according to any particular order nor arranged to make neat rows, and were instead packed together into disorganised groups.

It was quite the chore to make sure we didn't step on them as we ventured further in, but this disarray did let me get a good look at the headstones. Most of the pictures showed old people in traditional Chinese dress; the youngest-looking one I saw seemed like he had been in his mid-50s when he had croaked. I wondered why these people had used their most recent photos to represent themselves on their tombstones; I'd have figured that they'd want themselves remembered as they had looked in their prime, young and full of life.

The most interesting plot I saw was a joint one, a bed filled with stones and shared by a husband-and-wife pair who'd died within three months of one another. It looked to be the only twin burial plot I'd seen so far.

"Hey, *Ah Em*," I called out. "Look at this ... They were buried together."

"Come on, Jonathan, don't look at other people's graves," she brushed me off without even looking at the tomb I was pointing to.

"What's *Ah Kong*'s plot like?" I asked, leaving the deceased couple behind. "Where is it? Is it far?"

"We're almost there, don't worry."

"Does it look like these graves here?"

"You'll see ..."

"Does it have space for *Ah Ma* too?"

Jen and Frida gave me their most contemptuously evil eyes. Either *Ah Em* hadn't caught my last question, or she was pretending she hadn't.

"What?" I asked Jen, shrugging nonchalantly.

"Shut up, Jonathan," she hushed me. "You're asking for it."

"It was just a ..." They were off again before I could finish, so I kept the rest of my reply to myself. Kevin continued to lead the procession like a little emperor, and the rest of us followed him like a cortege of fawning courtiers, Uncle Ben and Michael hopping around like the royal fools they were and letting out apologetic squeals each time they accidentally glanced against a tomb that came too close to the path, often only to bump into another one on the other side.

When I looked back to the gateway we had entered through, it was a small hole in the distance. Ahead of us, the cemetery sloped downwards into another section, leading to newer-looking graves with more recent dates. Some of these graves appeared to have been recently visited and still carried the flowers, trinkets and freshly-burnt incense that had been left behind for the newly-dead by their families. This part of the cemetery looked twice as large as the first one had, and at the far end, the rest of our procession was gathered at *Ah Kong*'s plot.

I saw that it was a choice location, laid down on a slight elevation and set apart from the other graves by a generous distance. A frangipani tree stood over the site, offering a nice amount of shade to the grave as well as the people gathered by it.

We finally caught up with *Ah Peh*, Pa and *Ah Koh*, and I got my first up-close view of the gravesite: a concrete-lined pit set into a large, flat sheet of marble. A pulley-like device had *Ah Kong*'s coffin suspended directly above it, and a large pile of earth lay beside the grave; it was amazing to imagine that this massive load had been wheel-barrowed all the way in here, for surely no vehicle could have delivered it through the gateway and past all the tombs that we'd passed by to reach this part of the cemetery.

What was noticeably absent was a headstone for the tomb; I saw only a plain wooden board with an inscription, held up by a stand placed in front of the burial plot.

"Hey, how come it's just this?"

"They will build it afterwards," Pa answered. His bamboo staff had been put aside, as had *Ah Peh* and *Ah Koh*'s respective items.

"Why?"

"We don't build our graves before we're dead."

"Not even a ..."

"Quiet. They're lowering the coffin into the ground soon."

We gathered around the grave in silence as *Ah Peh* approached the funeral workers and had a word with them. He then addressed us, saying that *Ah Kong* was about to be laid to rest, and that we were to look away as the workers did it, just like we had when he'd been loaded into the hearse. Pa reiterated the message to Aaron and me, and then we fanned out, forming a semi-circular line around the grave. Our positions set, we all then turned our backs to the coffin. Moving my head ever so slightly to the right, I saw from the corner of my eyes as Frida, who was standing beside me, reached out to hold Kevin's hand, and then both of them looked on ahead with tears welling in their eyes. Standing on my other side was Jen, squinting stoically, her hand thankfully not extending towards mine.

It wasn't more than a minute when we were told we could face the burial site once again. The coffin was in its final resting place now, and the workers speedily moved the machinery out of the way. Several members of our group started to sniff loudly, and *Ah Peh*, sobbing, grabbed a handful of soil from the nearby pile and threw it into the pit. Pa, still stone-faced as ever, and *Ah Koh* joined in, and then the rest of us followed suit, throwing in clumps of dirt that rained atop the coffin lid in quiet thuds and splatters. The sole exception was Kevin, who tearfully poured in the ashes from the basin he was carrying, scattering them onto *Ah Kong*'s casket. My feet placed close to the edge, I crouched and peered at the coffin inside for one last look. Covered in the earth we'd just pelted at it, it lay nestled in there like a book at the bottom of an old trunk, the story over and never to be read again.

Standing close to the plot was a round and wide brick brazier as high as my waist, with a metal grille positioned halfway along its height. As per *Ah Peh*'s orders, after we'd all done a couple of throws and Kevin had emptied the basin, we went over to this brazier to carry out the last part of the funeral. There, we grandchildren started lining the grille with the paper ingots we'd brought along, using up about one sack's worth in the process, and then we set fire to them. The strategy was to let the flames consume the bulk of the ingots before we added any more, so as to avoid having to continually face the high temperatures and smoke created by the pyre of paper offerings. The first heat wave that we generated was the result of not abiding by these rules, and I took it in my face full-on, being too slow to get out of the way. The flash was searing, but not as much a problem as the cloud of dirty grey soot that accompanied it, sending me into a retching fit.

After we had wisened up to the process, the burning of the ingots turned out a mildly enjoyable exercise, and Aaron and I even had a race to see who could finish off the bag we were sharing. We should've felt remorseful watching something that we'd slaved over for days get destroyed before our eyes in mere seconds, yet, strangely, the only thing we felt was a great deal of satisfaction in seeing it all get reduced to cinders. When we were done with our complete supply of ingots, we packed up the now-empty plastic bags and departed together, leaving behind the workers to finish with the burial. We walked all the way down the hill and back to the driveway of the deserted house where we had parked the minibus; Pa, *Ah Peh* and *Ah Koh* climbed in with us this time, along with their funeral artifacts. The seating got rearranged slightly, owing to the extra passengers, and Michael, Aaron and me ended up at the bus's rear.

"Okay, we're heading home now," *Ah Peh* announced. "Nobody look back, alright? Don't look back at the road going up the cemetery."

"Why not?" I called out.

"Just don't, Jonathan!" my uncle cried. "Otherwise, you might get taken away with *Ah Kong*."

"Really? But how will ..."

"Don't argue with us," Pa flashed me a steely glare. "Just do as we tell you to, okay?" The driver hit the ignition, and we began to pull out of the driveway and towards the main road.

"How long before we can look back again?" Aaron asked me quietly, eyes directed forwards.

"I don't know ... Never, I guess."

"What? Never?"

"Yes, you'll always have to avert your eyes every time you pass by this place," I whispered. "Or *Ah Kong*'s ghost will latch on to your back and never let go."

"You're lying. I'm asking Pa."

"Should I turn around now? I'm sure I could try," I teased him.

"No, don't! What if you get taken away?"

"You'll inherit my toys, right? Why should you care?"

This made my brother pause for thought.

"You're actually thinking about it. Ha! You want me to get

taken away, don't you?"

"Guys, shut up!" griped Michael, putting his head against the windowpane. "You're giving me a headache."

I ignored him and turned back to my younger brother.

"If you get taken away, can I have your books?" asked Aaron. "Don't give them to Michael."

"Why the hell would I want this loser's books?" our eldest sibling muttered under his breath.

"Yeah, Michael wouldn't be able to understand them anyway. He'd need something easier," I replied to Aaron. "Like your old *My First Alphabet* or *The Counting Donkey* or ..."

I was suddenly grabbed from the side by my neck, in a chokehold. "Who's the smart one now?" Michael jeered, squeezing me tightly.

"I don't know," I spluttered. "The one who knows what's zero minus two hundred dollars?"

He didn't take too kindly to that, and upped the pressure. I twisted and turned in a fruitless attempt to strike back against him, but succeeded only in causing enough of a ruckus to draw the attention of everyone else in the bus towards us. We received some blustering outrage from Pa and Jen, a measured warning from *Ah Peh*, and squeamish implorations from Uncle Ben. Nothing doing; Michael remained relentless.

And yet, even as I struggled to break free from the wrestling move my brother had most probably stolen from one of those cheesy TV shows he watched, and even as I attempted to block out the threats of serious repercussions we were receiving from the adults for the tussle we'd got ourselves in, I couldn't help but feel that, for the first time in a long while, *this* was where I was supposed to be, fitting in as perfectly as my head did inside the crook of my brother's elbow.

The funeral was over and finally, I was going home.

Chapter Sixteen

The first thing Pa did when we returned to the house was to drag Michael and me away for our customary earful. He did this out of the earshot of the rest of the family, which was a bewildering move on his part for it was done solely to spare us some embarrassment. We were then dismissed to join the others, who were lined up in front of a bucket of water sitting at the edge of the house's front porch. Out in the garden, workers were busy disassembling the tent and putting the chairs away. The platform and altar were gone, and it looked like the house would have been cleared of all traces of *Ah Kong*'s funeral by the afternoon.

I circumvented the queue to see the ritual up close. The water had a number of freshly-picked leaves floating on its surface, a few of which got drawn up in the pail *Ah Peh* used to scoop from the much larger bucket. He splashed the water onto his face and arms, tipped a bit more over his head, and then entered the house. *Ah Em* was next after him, but before I could watch her pour the water onto herself, Pa pulled me away.

"It's for cleansing the spirit. With blessed water," he muttered. "Now, wait your turn to wash with it."

And so to the end of the line I went. When my turn came, I rinsed myself twice-over as a precaution, just to make sure that no ghost would latch on to my back or my feet or any other part of my body, and then I entered the house to join the others. They were gathered in the living room, listening as *Ah Em* reminded us to change out of our mourning outfits promptly so that the funeral organisers could take them back to the local temple without delay. We got that done, and then dumped the clothes in a pile in the middle of the room, where *Ah Kong*'s body had laid only yesterday, before going into the kitchen for a quick lunch.

As per traditional funeral customs, the visiting families, Pa's and *Ah Koh*'s, had to leave the house and return to their respective homes before sunset. It was still around midday, and there really was no rush, but Pa seemed keen on getting out of the house as soon as possible, hassling Aaron and me into finishing our food quickly and sending us upstairs to pack. Still hungry, we went on our way with a few extra sandwiches in tow. As we climbed up the stairwell, we caught sight of Pa pulling Michael away for a private discussion.

"What's happening? Are they fighting again?" Aaron whispered to me worriedly.

"Maybe," I whispered back. If that was the case, hopefully Pa would go a bit easy on our brother this time around.

I needed only about a minute to organise my stuff, and then watched as Aaron dumped his stuff in my bag before he zoomed off for a much-needed toilet break. While I finalised our packing, Kevin spun about in his swivel chair and idly watched me work.

"Got all your homework done?" he asked.

"Oh, crap. No." I didn't need to be reminded of it now. Apart from the half-finished maths papers, I had plenty of incomplete work for other subjects left back at my place, as well as all the extra reading I was meant to be doing for the topical tests.

"I'll do it when I get home," I sighed.

"Yeah. It's not like you have a choice," Kevin said with a

smirk. I could see that my cousin was getting back to his normal self.

"Right. So, how's your back doing, Kevin? You feeling better?" I forced a sarcastic grin.

Kevin grinned back. "Hey, you were right. The Malacca Lady is full of crap. I can't believe I got so scared of her."

"Of course I was right."

"I still got this with me though. Just in case." He pointed to the red *hu* he was wearing, the one the Lady had given him to ward off ghosts.

"By the way, your friend Radzi messaged me," he informed. "I had to change the SIM cards back myself because your lazy-ass brother couldn't be bothered to."

"Oh, yeah, Radzi ..." I felt a bit guilty that I'd forgotten to send my friend some form of reassurance that I'd made it back home yesterday. "Just message him back. Say I'll call him from my house later."

Nice as it was to hear from my friend, this also served as another terrifying reminder of my inevitable return to school tomorrow. This was the very reason my least favourite time of the week was Sunday evening, and why I hated the final day of any holiday, when all my prior enjoyment was wiped out by the dreaded anticipation of another fresh week of boredom and torture.

I then noticed that Kevin was fiddling with something in between his fingers.

"What's that? Another charm the Malacca Lady gave you?"

"This?" He showed me a small piece of cloth about the size of a milk cracker, in a similar shade of blue to the funeral clothes we'd been wearing over the last few days. "Nope. My dad gave this to me. He said we have to wear this for forty days. Pinned to our school uniforms."

"Why?"

"It's the rules. My dad said we have to."

"Where're ours then?"

"I don't know. Ask your father."

I immediately popped downstairs to do just that. Also I wanted to subtly hint at the possibility of buying some takeaway on our way home. A celebration felt warranted; after all, I had a call from Mum to look forward to today. At least that's what Pa had promised me.

The ground-floor living room was deserted when I got there. The kitchen ought to have been my next choice, but instead, I went in the opposite direction to search in the other rooms. I walked towards *Ah Ma*'s room first, sneaking up to its slightly ajar door to listen for any traces of my father inside. After about a minute of failing to detect any signs of activity, I opened the door fully and entered the room.

It was empty, so I decided to leave. But as I was about to, I realised that I could hear the strains of a conversation taking place outside the house, on the porch just beyond the room's outer wall. I crept over to the window to get a better listen of the muffled voices, all the while bending down and keeping my head just below the sill.

"Maybe it won't turn out that way ..."

That sounded like Uncle Ben.

"Not so loud," *Ah Koh* replied, her voice softer and harder to pick out. "And besides, who is she staying with, hmm? Don't tell me you can't put two and two together?"

"You can't make assumptions like that."

"Ooh, that woman drives me so mad. The nerve of her and her family ... If only my father had listened to me before he ... Now, he's just gone and thrown it all away ..."

"Honey, you're overreacting ..."

"Overreacting? Who do you think has my mother in the palm of her hand, huh? Who gets to be around her 24/7?"

"Sunshine ..."

"She's going to get my mother to hand everything over to her, can't you see that? One fine day, she'll just put her hand over my mother's and make her sign ... then it'll all be over. But I'm not giving up without a fight ... That's my money too and if she thinks she's getting all of it ..."

Their voices faded away, and another couple of seconds later, I heard car doors being opened and slammed shut. My aunt and uncle then left, apparently without a sending off by a member of the household.

I had never seen *Ah Koh* get so angry before. What was she so mad about? I had no idea, and I couldn't ask anyone about it anyway. Moving on, I exited *Ah Ma*'s room to continue the search for my father.

No sooner had I emerged from the room than the door to the one next to it flew open. Michael rushed past me in the direction of the stairs, while Pa remained standing at the room's doorway. This was the house's storeroom, so why had the two of them been talking in there? I peeped in and saw that a cardboard dollhouse was sitting atop a box in the room, designed in the style of an ancient Chinese mansion, with its walls painted in red and its roofing in green. Outside this miniature home were a few other cardboard miniatures, namely two small cars and a line of little figurines wearing uniforms to indicate their respective roles of cook, chauffeur, maid, and so on.

Pa closed the door before I could see any more of the room's contents.

"What's that?"

"That's for later," he glowered. "We'll send it up to your *Ah Kong* when we go back to his grave after the tombstone is done. So, are you ready to go?"

"Yeah, I guess ..."

He looked me up and down, unconvinced. "You don't look ready. Where's your watch? Did you lose it yesterday?"

I shook my head dumbly, unable to answer him.

"That was a very expensive watch, Jonathan. You'd better look for it," he said.

I nodded, wondering whether or not to tell him the truth about what I'd done to the watch. Fortunately, my father seemed to have already lost interest in the topic. "Okay, forget it. Just hurry up now, get your things down and call the others. We're leaving soon."

"Okay. By the way, Kevin had this blue cloth ..."

"Don't waste time!" he erupted. "Go now and get everyone to come downstairs!"

Given no time to make even the quickest query, I ran back upstairs. There, I saw that Michael was standing by one of the shelves outside Kevin's room and was staring into space.

"Hey," I called out to him. "You ready to leave? Where are we dropping you off at?" I figured I might not be seeing him for a while, so it was probably best to at least know where I'd be able to find him, on the unlikely chance of my having to go on another Michael-search in the future

"Hey, are you listening?" I yelled. My brother was still zoned out, seemingly deaf to my questions. "What's wrong with you? Pa tell you to go fly a kite about the two hundred dollars?"

That did the trick. He finally turned to look at me. "Buzz off, toadstool," he cursed, but without the usual passion.

"We're going home now. I don't know where you're going but …" I continued.

"Idiot. I'm coming home with you guys."

"What?" I'd never realistically expected Michael and Pa's reconciliation to last beyond the burial, let alone long enough for him to be allowed to return home with us.

"You're coming home? With us?"

"Pa asked me to."

"You've got to be joking."

"No. He freakin' said that I should come home and be with the rest of you guys."

"And you? You want to come home?"

"Yeah, well …" Michael looked both sheepish and exasperated. "I sorta do … I could use a better place to stay. I could use some money too. I'm so broke."

"Are you sure that's why? Or is it because you need a place to hide from all the people you've stolen stuff from. Mohidin can't be the only one."

"Shut up," he said, growing mad, pointing a finger at me. "You have the nerve to …"

"No, you shut up," I cut in. "The mess you're in now is all your own fault, and you aren't acting like you've even learnt your lesson. If you're back in the house, you'd better do yourself a favour and not be so stubborn with Pa like you were last time. It's his house and we live in it too, so don't you dare screw things up again, because we'll all be paying the price for it. Got it?"

Like yesterday, I left him at a loss for words and marched into Kevin's room. Inside, Aaron was just as shocked at Pa's change of heart, and just as miffed as I was about having to share the backseat with Jen on the ride back home. With our packing all done, we said our brief goodbyes to our cousin, and then headed downstairs to meet the adults at the front porch. *Ah Ma* was there too, bound to her wheelchair and adrift inside her own world like she usually was. We made our customary farewells to her, and then our uncle and aunt. *Ah Ma*, as usual, remained oblivious to us and made no meaningful response to our hugs or our goodbyes, while *Ah Peh* and *Ah Em* looked pretty smug with themselves over our father's reunion with Michael, as if they'd had an instrumental role in making it happen.

And that was it. Aaron, Jen and I were forced to cram into the back of the car as Michael sat himself in the front passenger seat, and then Pa pulled away to the sound of that same old CD spewing out his favourite soppy tunes. Having managed to nab a seat by the window, I leaned on to it, looking out at the familiar scenery flying past us as we drove on home. The hut constructed out of metal sheets was still there at Kampung Bukit Seri, but the tall tree that had accompanied it only a couple days ago was gone now, and in its place was a spindly, blunt-ended stump that rose about as high as the cars parked in its vicinity.

Jen was by the other window, texting on her phone, and Aaron was wedged in between us, reading that same old storybook from the ride to *Ah Peh*'s house.

"Jonathan?" Pa suddenly called out from the front.

"Yes?" Was my father actually initiating a conversation with me? Such an occurrence was unprecedented ... Had I stumbled upon that rarest of prizes, getting treated like a normal person by my father?

"Your Mum just texted. She can't call tonight. She's tired from the jetlag. Maybe next week when she's ... When she's feeling better."

"Oh. Okay."

No need to panic, I told myself. This was just a delay, a little hitch in the plan. She probably was genuinely jetlagged. Or maybe she was sick with something. Or busy making plans to finally open up that dance school of hers. In any case, it was just a few more days of wait. That was doable, no problem at all. In fact, the wait would only make that phone call all the more special, and this time around, I had a guarantee from my parents that it was definitely coming soon. So why worry?

I fished out my lucky pen from my pocket, and twirled it between my fingers. Now all I had to do was find something else to think about, so I could keep my mind off Mum. Surely an easy task for the most miserable boy in the whole world – I would just have to turn my attention to the next most pressing concern in my life ...

Which was clearly all the work that was due tomorrow when I got back to school. And the most burdensome of my tasks was the unfinished maths exercises, which were still far from completion.

Well, at least here was a problem I could do something about. And sort it out I would. Even if it meant staying up all night, foregoing the sleep I desperately needed after the eventful funeral.

And even if it meant doing those papers in an exam-style setting, with no help from the calculator.

And having to hand it in on time, with all of Mrs. Yap's rules obeyed to the letter – the questions would be copied on to fresh sheets of A4 paper; all workings would be neatly shown; one-line spacing would be provided in between each problem; the solutions would be underlined twice; the date would be written on the top right-hand corner; the fractions would have diagonal lines instead of horizontal ones; a margin spanning one centimetre from the left edge of each page would be drawn, with a ruler; a big enough gap would be left after the last answer for Mrs. Yap's comments and corrections.

And everything would be written in ...

Well ...

Written in black, obviously.

Disclaimer

This is a work of fiction. Although many of the places, situations and people in the story are inspired by my own personal experiences while growing up in Brunei, most of the location names are made up and this book is not meant to be regarded as autobiographical in any way, nor is it to be taken as a definitive description of day-to-day Bruneian life.

To the reader interested in learning more about Brunei, there is plenty of information available on the web for your perusal. Or better yet, you could go over and see for yourself.

Acknowledgements

Thanks to Monsoon Books, especially Phil and Sujatha for their help and advice on the book. Thanks to everyone else who had a look at the early drafts; the feedback is greatly appreciated.

Most of all, thanks to you, reader, for giving a boy and his humble world an audience.